"THAT'S WHAT I LIKE ABOUT YOU, ROMY." FOXX SMILED. "YOU DON'T BEAT AROUND THE BUSH."

"Not when I want something." Romy smiled at Foxx invitingly, and he moved to sit beside her on the bed. She turned her face to him and offered her lips. He met them with his, and her mouth opened to his. She sighed softly in her throat and Foxx released her.

"I don't know why we waited so long," she said. "But now that we've broken the ice . . ."

She stood up and began slowly unbuttoning her jacket. . . .

*Second in the FOXX Series
of quick and gripping, action-packed
Western adventure*

Other authentic tales of the Old West in Dell Editions:

FOXX'S GOLD

ZACK TYLER

A DELL BOOK

Published by
Dell Publishing Co., Inc.
1 Dag Hammarskjold Plaza
New York, New York 10017

Dell ® TM 681510, Dell Publishing Co., Inc.

ISBN: 0-440-13552-4

Printed in the United States of America
First printing—March 1981

FOXX'S GOLD

CHAPTER 1

Foxx stopped just outside the dim glow of the switch bull's-eye that made a tiny puddle of light in the coal-black darkness of the C&K sidings. Beyond the rows of tracks, the soft sighing of the Sacramento River's currents gave an overtone of sadness to the night as the river hesitated before going into the constricted banks of its bend below the town of Red Bluff.

Foxx had been carrying his twisted stogie in his cupped left hand to keep its glow from being visible. He bent down and took a final puff from the stogie before dropping it on the cinder-paved ground and grinding it out under his boot-heel.

Beside him, Tom Gerard asked in a whisper, "Why'd you stop, Foxx? You hear something up ahead?"

"No. Just wanted to get rid of my smoke before we get too close to that decoy string you set up. That's the siding right ahead of us, isn't it?"

"Yes. I put three cars out there yesterday, and

made sure the word got around that they'd been pulled off a highballing manifest because their journals were running hot."

"That ought to draw our man out, then."

"I'll buy the drinks if it doesn't," Gerard told his chief.

"That's one offer I'll take, regardless of whether this is a live stakeout or a waterhaul."

They waited in silence. Foxx rubbed his chin thoughtfully, drawing his fingers over the stubble that was already spouting on his jaws and cheeks below his close-trimmed sideburns.

He hadn't taken time to stop for a shave after Tom Gerard's wire had been handed him by the clerk in the San Francisco office. "Trap set," the wire had read. "Might spring it tonight. Could use help if possible." The Red Bluff freight station had been the recurring target of a persistent freight-car thief who seemed to have an uncanny knack of smelling out valuable loads. Foxx had suggested that Gerard set a trap for the thief, and had been half-expecting the message.

As chief of the detective division of the California and Kansas Railroad, Foxx took pride in moving at once when one of his division detectives notified him that an important case was drawing to a climax. He'd swung by his hotel to pick up his always-packed valise on the way to the ferry and rattled north in the caboose of a freight train up the Sacramento Valley branch of the C&K, arriving in Red Bluff in the early hours of the night.

Now Foxx asked Gerard, "You said in one of your reports you had a pretty good idea who this damn thief is. You ever get anything certain on it?"

"I'm sure I've got it narrowed down now to two

men, but the only way we'll ever get positive proof is to catch whoever it is while he's pulling a job."

"It's the best way. No room for a car thief to weasel out, if you catch him at work."

A scraping on the cinders ahead of them brought both men to tense attention. Gerard whispered, "You heard it, too, I guess?"

"Yes. Somebody's prowling up at the cars. You go right; I'll go left."

Wasting no time, they moved out. Like Foxx, Gerard was used to walking silently over the uncertain footing of a railroad yard. The knack of lifting their feet straight up and putting them straight down on the shifting cinders was the first move any good railroad detective mastered. After each of them had taken two or three steps, Foxx could no longer hear Gerard's movements, and he knew that the prowler who'd fallen into the trap the young division detective had set wouldn't be aware of their approach until it was too late for him to run.

From the darkness ahead a metallic snap broke the silence. Foxx recognized the noise at once. It was the breaking pop a car-door seal made when twisted off with a crowbar, sure sign that a car thief was after whatever loot the car might hold. He remembered Tom Gerard's remark about spreading the word that the three freight cars placed as decoys on the siding had been pulled off a manifest—the fast-running freights to which all railroads consigned the most valuable loads they hauled.

Another noise reached Foxx's ears—this time it was the broken scraping of a boxcar door sliding open. The thief had taken the bait, and they were sure now of catching him inside the car. Foxx waited for a moment before moving ahead to give the prowler plenty of time to get in the car.

He reached the end of the boxcar. There was barely enough light for him to see the black rectangle of the partly opened door and to make out a hint of Gerard's moving form as the young detective crept silently along the side of the car toward the opened door. Foxx waved for Gerard to slow down, to wait until the man in the boxcar showed a light. Gerard didn't see Foxx's signal, for he kept edging closer to the open door. Foxx moved to join him.

A match sputtered into flame inside the boxcar, followed by the yellow glow of a lantern. Foxx speeded up, but Gerard was at the open boxcar door by now. The young railroad detective had his gun out, and was framed in the open door against the light. Foxx was only a step away when the shot rang out, and Gerard slumped to the ground.

Foxx reached the door just as the man inside was blowing out the lantern. He had a momentary glimpse of a hard, ugly face as he drew and got off a fast shot, then the lantern guttered out. In the car, Foxx heard the thunk of a pistol dropping to the floor, followed by the crash of glass as the lantern fell. He levered himself into the boxcar's midnight-black interior and groped his way across the floor until his hand encountered cloth.

His exploring hand told Foxx his shot had found a mark. The thief lay still, but Foxx could hear the man breathing harshly. He pulled handcuffs from his belt and rolled the limp form over while he cuffed the thief's hands behind his back. Then he dropped from the car to see how badly Gerard had been hit.

When his fingers felt hot, slick blood on the young detective's face, Foxx clamped his jaws tightly. He struck a match to be sure. The thief's bullet had gone into one of Gerard's eyes. Tom Gerard had been dead before he hit the ground.

"Damn!" Foxx gritted between his teeth. "My fault, part of it. I wasn't fast enough to back him up."

Then, because there was nothing he could do to help Tom Gerard, Foxx turned his attention to the killer.

Foxx was not gentle with the handcuffed man he prodded down Red Bluff's still-sleeping main street toward the Tehama County Courthouse a little more than an hour later. He'd wasted no time in extracting the killer-thief's name from him after making sure his snap shot had only grazed the man, and it suited Foxx very well that there were no curious onlookers to ask questions. At the moment, he wanted nothing more than to get Buck Yeager into the hands of the sheriff and out of his sight.

Dawn had crept into the sky before he'd finished questioning Yeager, but the day was still very young. Across the Sacramento River the pink of sunrise was just tingeing a line of thin, low clouds above the ragged edge of the sandstone rise that gave the town its name. There were a few stevedores moving around at the steamboat landing, but the wide, unpaved street itself was deserted.

Yeager stumbled on a loose sidewalk board, unbalanced by the position of his arms, which the handcuffs kept pulled behind him, and Foxx unceremoniously grabbed the chain linking the cuffs and pulled him erect.

"Keep to your feet, Yeager," he snapped coldly. "Don't try any of your tricks on me. I don't make the kind of mistakes Tom Gerard did."

"Damn it, I can't help it if I hit a loose board," Yeager protested sullenly. "Any more than I could help your man getting in the way of my slug."

"Shut up and keep walking," Foxx commanded. "If you remind me one more time that you killed Tom, I just might forget about turning you over to the sheriff and take care of you myself."

Yeager looked over his shoulder, but turned his head away quickly when he saw the smoldering anger that had turned Foxx's brown eyes into an ominous midnight-black.

Yeager was a big man, bigger even than Foxx. His face had never been one to inspire confidence, and now he looked meaner than ever. His appearance wasn't improved by the swollen, angry red line of the bullet from Foxx's Smith & Wesson that had creased his cheekbone during the exchange of shots along the C&K sidings that bordered the high-water mark of the river on the outskirts of the town.

They passed the hotel, its fat white columns rosy now in the morning light that gave a deeper hue to the building's redbrick walls. A white-jacketed porter was sweeping the hotel porch; he looked curiously at Foxx and Yeager, but said nothing. Across the street ahead of them, the courthouse loomed. Its windows were dark except for one on the side of the building at the ground-floor level.

Foxx twisted the chain of the handcuffs and steered Yeager into the street at an angle that would take them to the building. He swung his prisoner to one side to open the door, then shoved Yeager uncere-

moniously through it, into the sheriff's office. Sheriff
Carlson was halfway across the room when Foxx
pushed Yeager inside. The short, pudgy sheriff was
buckling on his gunbelt. He looked past Yeager to
Foxx.

"Well," Carlson said, relief in his voice. "I guess
it was you and your boys doing the shooting down
at the yards?"

"It was," Foxx nodded.

"My night man sent word over to the house that
there'd been gunfire," the sheriff explained. "Took
him a little while to find somebody to send, or I'd've
got to the yards in time to give you a hand. But it
don't look like you needed much help."

"We managed," Foxx replied.

"Buck Yeager!" Carlson said, inspecting Foxx's
prisoner. "I sorta wondered if he didn't have a hand
in them robberies Tom told me about down at the
C&K yards." He looked beyond Foxx and Yeager to
the door that still stood open. "Tom bringing somebody else along?"

"Tom's dead."

Carlson's jaw dropped. "The hell you say!"

Foxx jerked his head to indicate Yeager. "You can
book him for the murder. And the robberies, too,
just as soon as he signs his name to a confession. Not
that he'll stand trial for them, unless your jury up
here gets soft-headed and lets him off on the murder
charge."

"There's not much chance of that," Carlson said
confidently. "Anybody from here that sits on a jury
is going to know what kind of man Yeager is. They'd
be more apt to organize a necktie party when word
gets around."

"No. Much as I liked Tom, I wouldn't want to see that happen. Neither would my bosses. Let the court handle him."

"He'll get what's coming to him, Foxx. You can be sure about that." The sheriff hesitated, then asked, "You need any help from us in—well, in fixing for Tom to be laid away?"

"Thanks for your offer, but the C&K takes care of its own. I roused a couple of men out of the gandy-dancer shack. They're wheeling Tom's body into town to the undertaker's on a baggage cart."

Yeager had stood in sullen silence while Foxx and the sheriff talked. Now he grumbled, "Listen, these damn cuffs you put on me are cutting my wrists up. How about taking 'em off, so I can get some feeling back in my hands?"

"You can wear 'em until your hands drop off, for all I care," Foxx replied. He turned to Carlson. "He's yours now, Sheriff."

Carlson waited while Foxx unlocked the handcuffs, then took Yeager by the arm. He led the killer to the inner door and called, "Bert! Come get this yahoo and put him away until I can talk to the District Attorney about him." When the jailer had taken Yeager in charge, the sheriff stepped back to Foxx. "We'll keep him tight, Foxx. You can put him outa your mind."

"I sure don't want to think about him," Foxx said. He pulled a single-action Colt from his waistband and handed it to Carlson. "Yeager's gun. You'll need it for evidence, I suppose."

"I suppose." The sheriff hefted the weapon and said thoughtfully, "Glad as I am to see Buck Yeager finished, I sure wish it had been for something else."

"So do I," Foxx agreed. "Tom Gerard alive was worth a lot more to me and to the C&K than Yeager is in jail. Tom was a good friend, and one of my best men. Due for promotion to central office, the first job that came open there." He shook his head. "Well, I'm going to stop by the depot, and then go over to the hotel and get some sleep. It's been a long night, and not a very good one."

At the C&K depot-station, Foxx stopped long enough to ask the stationmaster to arrange for Gerard's funeral. Then he went to the dispatcher's cubbyhole and sent a message to Jim Flaherty, chief of the C&K's railroad police force, informing him of Gerard's death. Wording the message made him even gloomier than he'd been before. He still blamed himself in part for Gerard's death. A drink of old bourbon before breakfast gave him no appetite for food. He pushed his plate of eggs and bacon away after a few bites and went up to his room, hoping that some sleep would improve his disposition.

A soft rasping of metal against metal roused Foxx from his restless doze. The years of his youth, when he was reared by the Comanches to become a member of their tribe, had taught him to wake instantly, with all his senses alert.

"Who is it?" he called.

There was a moment of silence from the door; the grating of the key in the lock stopped. Then a woman's voice answered, "It's the maid, sir. Doing the rooms."

"Well, come back and do this one later, after I check out."

"Yes, sir."

Foxx relaxed. He was settling back against the pillow when the key scraped again. There was something wrong about the noise. To Foxx's keen ears, it didn't sound like a key being withdrawn from a lock, but like the bolt was being turned. Woman's voice or not, instinct set Foxx into motion. He rolled off the bed, reaching as he moved for the holstered pistol that he'd placed on a chair beside the bed.

He had the revolver in his hand, still holstered, and was on his feet between the chair and the bed when the door banged open, thudded against the bedroom wall, and in the instant that it was still swinging Foxx got a glimpse of a white-clad woman framed in the opening, a pistol leveled in her hand.

Foxx dropped as the gun barked. A fluff of feathers spurted up from the pillow where his head had been a moment earlier. The chair kept him from getting a clear view of the woman as she turned to run. On the floor, cramped in the narrow space between bed and chair, the chair legs between him and the door restricting his movements, Foxx had no chance to fire.

Along the corridor doors began opening and voices sounded. Foxx was on his feet the instant the woman vanished, pulling on his trousers. He stepped into his boots, jamming his feet in them while he pulled the Smith & Wesson out of its holster.

He didn't stop for a shirt, or to strap on his gunbelt, but ran out of the room down the short flight of stairs to the lobby, and looked around for his would-be assassin. The woman was nowhere in sight, but the heads of the half-dozen men in the lobby were still turned in the direction of the door leading to the street.

Taking his cue from the turned heads, Foxx trotted through the lobby and outside. He stopped on the long narrow veranda that ran the width of the hotel, and stood between two of its fat white columns while he looked both ways along the street.

By now it was late morning, and there were people walking along the board sidewalks, a buggy or two and a wagon moving along the street, a few horsemen cutting in and out between the vehicles. Across the street and a dozen yards down from the hotel on the sidewalk, Foxx saw the flash of a white dress.

It was the only white garment visible. He stepped off the veranda and started down the street on the hotel side, following the only clue in sight. The woman wearing the dress was moving swiftly, and Foxx half-ran, half-trotted, dodging around the slower-moving pedestrians on the narrow board sidewalk as he tried to catch up.

A brewery wagon piled high with kegs trundled between Foxx and his quarry. When the wagon passed, the woman in the white dress had vanished. Foxx crossed the street quickly, looking as he moved, trying to decide into which of the two store doors the woman had gone. One of the stores bore a sign, RODGERS' FASHION EMPORIUM; the sign over the second read MILLHOUSE GROCERIES. With a mental shrug, Foxx chose the dress shop.

He pushed inside, unmindful of his touseled hair and the fact that the stubble on his jaws had darkened during the hours that had passed since the stakeout at the siding, forgetting that he'd pulled on his trousers but no shirt. There were two or three customers in the shop, women, being attended by a middle-aged man and a young woman clerk. All of them gasped when they saw Foxx, and one of the women let out a stifled shriek.

Foxx asked the man, "Did a woman in a white dress come in here a minute ago?"

His eyes wide, a baffled look on his face, the man shook his head. Foxx nodded and ran out and into the store next door. It was deserted except for a denim-aproned clerk standing behind the long wooden counter. The man was staring along the counter toward the back of the store when Foxx entered. He turned and his eyes bulged at the sight of Foxx's pistol.

"What's going—" the clerk began.

Foxx interrupted. "A woman in a white dress. Did she come in here?"

For a moment the man hesitated, his eyes darting nervously to the aisle between the counter and the laden shelves behind it. Then he shook his head.

"N—no," he stammered. "I didn't see anybody at all come in, mister."

Foxx's fine-honed instinct told him to believe the clerk's nervousness instead of the man's words. He asked, "Are you real sure about that?"

"Sure, I'm sure. I guess I'd've seen anybody come in, wouldn't I? I been right here all the time." At the same time, the clerk's eyes kept moving back and forth, from Foxx to the end of the long counter.

Foxx laid the forefinger of his free hand across his lips and raised his thick eyebrows questioningly. The clerk nodded somewhat reluctantly. His eyes were still bulging wide and darting nervously between Foxx and the counter. Foxx returned the clerk's nod, trying to reassure the man.

"Guess she must've gone in the store next door, then."

Without moving from his place, Foxx raised and lowered his feet, letting them thud to the wooden floor less and less noisily. He stopped the in-place pacing and waited. The clerk looked as though he wanted to run, but could think of nowhere to run to.

Foxx's wait was not a long one. A moment ticked off and then another before there was a stir halfway down the counter and the woman in white stood up. Her arms dangled at her sides, a pistol clutched in her right hand. She gave a jump like a startled animal when she saw Foxx standing in front of the counter, his revolver leveled at her.

Speaking softly, trying not to startle her, Foxx said, "Open your hand and let that gun drop, ma'am. I don't want to have to shoot you."

For a split second Foxx thought the woman was going to obey his command. Then her eyes flickered and she brought her weapon up deliberately. Foxx had scruples about shooting a woman. He shifted his revolver muzzle to send a shot past her head. The slug tore into a shelf of airtights on the back wall, bursting some of the cans and sending a spattering of tomato pulp and juice over the woman's white dress.

Foxx saw the knuckle of her forefinger grow white as the finger tightened on the trigger. He dropped just before the gun in her hand spat its red spurt of muzzle-blast, and lead sang past Foxx's head as he hit the floor. This bullet landed in a stack of flour sacks, powdering Foxx with white dust.

He rolled just in time. Her second shot ripped into the floor where he'd been lying, raising a shower of pine splinters. Foxx changed the direction of his movement, scrambling close to the counter where he'd no longer be a target.

Another shot plowed into the floor, then still another into the edge of the counter above Foxx's head. When he heard the dull click of her revolver's hammer on an empty chamber, Foxx stood up.

"Now you've got an empty gun there," he said persuasively. "I guess it's time for you to put it down on the counter. Then maybe we can have a peaceful talk so I can find out what all this is in favor of."

Instead of obeying, the woman in white hurled the revolver at Foxx's head. He ducked. It sailed past him and clattered to the floor as the woman ran toward the end of the long counter.

Foxx ran after her and caught her easily before she could reach the counter's end. He vaulted the wooden top and grabbed her.

For a moment she fought like a wildcat. Her fingers raked Foxx's face, one of her nails digging a scratch in his cheek. He let his pistol drop and with both hands managed to grab her wrists and hold her still. She kicked at his shins, fighting with a silent ferocity that startled him. Foxx had seen Comanche squaws fight that way, but never a white woman.

Finally, by pulling on her wrists, he wrestled her to the floor and held her wrists imprisoned in one hand while he mopped away the blood from his scratched cheek with the other. He called to the clerk, "Get me a piece of rope or cord or something to tie her hands with!"

Still recovering from shock, the clerk finally brought a hank of thick twine. Foxx wrapped it around the woman's wrists until he was sure there were enough laps to hold her and tied the knot. During all this time she'd said nothing, but kept her lips tightly compressed, her breath whistling through her distended nostrils.

Foxx lifted her to her feet and turned her around to face him. He looked at her closely. In spite of her glowering, angry face, she was not ugly or completely unattractive. Her eyes were filled with tears of frustration, and her too-thin lips still twisted in a half-snarl. Her face was thin, and though she was not old, she showed the furrows of premature wrinkles on her brow and at the corners of her mouth.

"Now, then," he said, holding back his anger, "you might as well tell me what kind of grudge you're carrying."

"All I need to tell you is my name," she spat. "I might as well, because if I don't, you'll find it out easy enough. I'm Annie Yeager."

"Buck Yeager's wife?" Foxx frowned.

She nodded. "You put my man in jail, and on a hanging charge. Now I guess you'll put me in with him."

"You sure guessed right, Mrs. Yeager," Foxx told her. "And I don't see much reason to put it off. I've still got some business here because of your husband. A funeral to go to, for one thing. It's just a step from here over to the courthouse, so we might as well get on with it. After I've gone, the sheriff can do what he wants to about you. But I'll feel a lot better if I know you're safe in a cell by your husband as long as I'm in Red Bluff."

CHAPTER 2

Foxx stood on the upper deck in the bow of the blunt-nosed ferryboat, puffing a stogie and watching the wall of fog that hid San Francisco's hills. The sun was just dipping below the top of the fogbank, its brightness being slowly obscured as the fine mist swallowed it bit by bit. The ferry plunged into the fog, and suddenly the air changed from mildly warm to unpleasantly chilly.

Buttoning his coat, Foxx settled his black homburg a bit lower on his head. From left and right the foghorns were blatting mournfully, the pilot guiding the ferry by ear now, setting the boat's course according to the volume of the foghorns' intermittent wails. The whistle of the ferry began adding its warning voice to the toots from other boats that crept through the fine mist on all sides.

As the ferry drew closer to its slip, the fog thinned at the water level, lifted by the layer of warm air that still lay close to the ground. The grayness of the afternoon fitted Foxx's state of mind. The scratch on his cheek made by Annie Yeager's fingernails had scabbed over and was beginning to itch irritatingly, and he hadn't been exactly cheerful at any time since Tom Gerard's funeral the day before. He still blamed himself in part for the young detective's death, but he hadn't expected Gerard to be in such a hurry to close in on the boxcar thief.

Foxx had wanted to get out of Red Bluff right after the funeral, but Sheriff Carlson had pulled him to one side at the cemetery and started talking about the evidence and testimony that would be needed at Buck Yeager's trial.

They hadn't finished their discussion before the service started, and had resumed their talk later. By the time Foxx had satisfied Carlson on all the points the sheriff raised, he'd missed the early evening's southbound freight. Resigning himself to the inevitable, he'd spent another night in Red Bluff and caught the morning passenger train south.

Under Foxx's feet the planking of the ferry's deck trembled as the boat slowed, preparing to nudge into its slip. He tossed the stub of his stogie into the curl of water raised by the blunt prow, and started for the lower deck to be ready to disembark.

Still absorbed in his unhappy thoughts, and back now in familiar surroundings, Foxx paid little attention to the crowd clustering around the end of the gangplank as he stepped off to the slip. There was always a crowd waiting when one of the cross-bay ferries docked. He began weaving through the knot of passengers waiting to board, and when a hand came to rest on his arm, reacted with a surprised start.

"You didn't expect I'd be here to meet you, did you, Foxx?" Vida Martin asked.

She smiled up at him, white teeth framed between soft, full lips, her green eyes sparkling. Foxx's gloom vanished as he looked at her. Vida was wearing a suit of broadcloth in a soft green that matched her eyes. The tailored coat draped closely around her voluptuous bust and undulated over her full hips in a manner that gave only a hint of the body beneath the cloth. Foxx thought of that body as he bent to kiss her and felt her muscles tighten as their lips touched.

He said, "I sure didn't. How'd you know when I was due back?"

"I had dinner with Clara and Caleb last night," she explained. Clara, Vida's older sister, was the wife of Caleb Petersen, the C&K Railroad's president and founder.

Vida went on, "Caleb told us about the trouble you'd run into up in Red Bluff, and I knew enough to look up the timetables and find out when you'd be most likely to get in. You've been away too much, Foxx. If I hadn't known from what Clara passed on to me, things Caleb had told her, I've gotten the idea you were avoiding me."

"Now, you know I'd never think of doing that, Vida. It just seems like the C&K's had a lot of trouble lately."

"Is your job always like that, Foxx? Chasing dynamiters all the way across Nevada, then before we've even had time to say hello, rushing up to Red Bluff. We haven't spent as much time together as I'd like."

"My kind of work's not like a clerk in an office,

or a floorwalker in a department store. I've got to
go where the trouble is, Vida. You know that."

"Oh, I'm not complaining, Foxx. But you're my
tonic, after all the months I've been by myself. I
want to be with you."

They reached the end of the ferry slip and started
across Last Street toward Market. Foxx said, "I'll
hail a hack. One thing I don't need right now is any
more walking."

"I told the hackman who brought me here to wait,"
Vida said. She looked at the row of carriages lined
up at the Market Street corner and pointed one out
to Foxx. "That's it. I thought we might have dinner
together, if you're not too tired."

"You know me better than that by now, Vida.
There's not any kind of time when I'd be too tired
for you." Foxx handed her into the carriage. To the
hackie he said, "Cosmopolitan Hotel." He got in and
told Vida, "We'd better stop by the hotel first. I
need a bath and some fresh clothes."

"Of course. Why do you think I met you, Foxx?
It's too early for dinner, anyhow. You'll enjoy the
evening more after you've bathed and changed."

They settled back on the leather seat, sitting close
together in the intimacy of lovers who have been
apart, as the hackman wheeled his vehicle around in
a tight circle and started back up Market Street.

Vida turned her face up for Foxx's kiss, a longer
and more prolonged caress than his kiss of greeting
on the dock. When their lips parted, she looked with
a frown at Foxx's face and reached a finger up to
trace the angry red scab that ran down his cheek.

"Caleb didn't say anything about you getting hurt,"
she said, her brow still furrowed.

"That's not anything to worry about," Foxx told her. "It's just a little scratch."

"From a woman's fingernails, at a guess," she said, then added quickly, "not that I'm jealous."

"Not that you'd have any reason to be," Foxx replied. "But you made a good guess. She was a little bit crazy. I'd just put her husband in jail for killing Tom Gerard, and she was out to get even with me."

"It sounds like a long story. You can tell me all about it later. Unless you'd rather not talk about it."

"Maybe it'd help if I told you. I keep thinking it might've been partly my fault that Tom got killed."

"Later, then. Right now, I'd like to have you all to myself for a while."

"Now, that's the nicest thing anybody's said to me for quite a spell. But I don't have to tell you, I feel the same way."

With a creaking of harness leather, the carriage stopped in front of the Cosmopolitan. Foxx gave Vida his hand to the sidewalk, and paid the hackman. They walked arm in arm through the deserted lobby and up the stairs to his two-room suite. Foxx locked the door and when he turned around, Vida was waiting. They clung together in a long caress, her full breasts crushed to his chest, her hand clutching at his crotch, feeling him begin to come erect. She pulled away from him reluctantly.

"Don't you think you should show a guest your rooms before you start getting her to the point where she's only interested in your bed?" she asked with a smile.

"There's not much to see. I don't spend a lot of time here, like you reminded me back at the ferry slip."

"Oh, I was just making a bad joke, Foxx. I don't have any strings on you, and you don't have any on me. We agreed from the beginning it'd be that way."

"That's how you said you wanted it."

"And I meant it. Still do. Now, let's forget what I said at the dock. I want to look around."

Foxx waved a hand to encompass the room. "Go ahead and look all you want to. But you sure won't find anything fancy. I'll fix us something to drink while you're looking."

Vida took in the Spartan furnishings of the sitting room in a single glance and wandered into the bedroom. Foxx opened the cellarette that stood on the side table and took out bottles and glasses. Though he preferred well-aged bourbon, straight, he kept a soda syphon on hand for visitors who preferred their drinks diluted. He tilted the bottle over a tall glass and added a squirt of the charged water for Vida, then poured his own drink in a tumbler.

Carrying the glasses, he joined Vida in the bedroom. She was standing in front of the opened closet door, her eyes fixed on the lines of boots on its floor. Foxx set the drinks on the dresser and went to look over her shoulder.

"You told me you liked nice boots," she smiled. "You didn't say anything about being a boot collector."

"Well, now, you wouldn't expect me to wear the same boots every day, would you? Any more'n you'd put on the same dress day in and day out?"

"Some of these are really beautiful, Foxx!" she exclaimed, bending down to run her hands over the gleaming leather tops of the fanciest ones. "I had no idea there were so many kinds!"

"It just happens I do like boots," he said. "Some folks collect paintings or statues, but what I enjoy more than things like that is good tanned leather, something I can like and get some good out of, too."

"After seeing these, I can't say I blame you." She closed the door of the closet and peered into the bathroom. "A magnificent bathroom, for a hotel. I don't think I've ever seen a tub that big before."

"That tub's one of the main reasons I keep on staying here at the Cosmopolitan Hotel. There's newer and fancier places been put up since I moved in, but I like a tub I can stretch out in full-length and not have to sit all squinched up with my knees out of the water. Which reminds me, the main reason we come up here was so I could take a bath and put on fresh clothes. These I got on are about ready to walk by themselves."

"I'll start your bath," Vida said. Then, with her eyes gleaming mischievously, she added, "With a tub that big, it's a waste of water for you to bathe alone. I might just share it with you, if you don't object too much."

"A man'd have to be crazy to turn down an offer like that. Go ahead. We can have our drinks while the tub's filling."

Foxx went back to the bedroom. He took off his shirt before remembering his drink on the dresser. Lighting a stogie, he sipped the rich whiskey appreciatively. In the bathroom, he could hear water gushing into the big six-foot-long tub.

Vida came in from the bathroom carrying her coat and shirtwaist. Her soft shoulders gleamed white, their symmetry broken only by the straps of her slip. Foxx handed her the whiskey and soda and went to the bed. He toed the bootjack from its place under the bed and sat down to take off his boots. Watching him from the dresser, her drink at her lips, Vida laughed suddenly, then coughed as she swallowed the wrong way.

Foxx jumped up and hurried to her. By the time he'd gotten to her side, the coughing fit had ended and she was chuckling. He asked, "Are you sure you're all right?"

"Of course I am." She put her glass on the dresser and took Foxx's hand, pulling him into her arms. "I was just remembering what happened the first time we were together, how you had to push my bottom with your foot while I held on to your boots."

"And a mighty pretty bottom it is," Foxx told her. "Even if I don't know whether it's prettier than what I'm looking at now."

He nuzzled the straps of her shift off one shoulder and then the other, and rubbed his face against her soft skin. His hands were busy pulling the top of her shift down to free her breasts. Then his lips moved to the rosettes that stood out like pink rose petals on her firm, full breasts.

As he continued to caress her, Vida's body tensed, then began to quiver. She unbuttoned Foxx's linen singlet until his belt stopped her, then unbuckled the belt and slid singlet and trousers off him. Her hands stroked Foxx's back for a moment, then moved down to grasp his growing erection.

"If we're going to bathe," she whispered, "we'd better do it now. In another minute or two, I'm going to want to share more than just a bath with you."

"I don't see a thing wrong with that," Foxx told her.

He fumbled at the clasp of her skirt until he solved its secret and lifted Vida off her feet. Skirt and shift slid free, but he had to put her down again while he worked her knickers over her flared hips. The dresser was just behind them. Vida took a half step back; Foxx lifted her to the dresser-top.

Vida offered her lips and Foxx met them with his own. They clung together in a long kiss, and while their tongues were still entwining, Foxx felt her hand at his groin, grabbing him and pulling him to her. He moved closer and when the soft, dry warmth of Vida's hand gave way to the greater warmth and wetness of her second lips, he went into her, burying himself fully in a single swift thrust.

"Ahh!" Vida sighed. "This is what I've missed all the time you've been away. Hold me this way for a few minutes, now, Foxx. I want to enjoy just having you inside me, filling me up."

Foxx remained motionless for a few moments, pressing firmly against Vida's yielding flesh. When she stirred and her eyes opened, he began to thrust in a slow, gentle rhythm. Vida rolled from side to side as he stroked, her back arching as she tried to take him in deeper.

"Wait," she whispered.

Foxx stopped his thrusting. She leaned back, bending her knees to bring them under Foxx's arms and then raised her legs high, her calves resting on his shoulders.

"Now!" she urged. "Hard and fast, Foxx!"

Foxx drove. Vida grabbed his biceps and pulled herself to him. Her breasts pushed between her spread thighs so that the coarsely matted hair on Foxx's wide chest rasped their protruding tips as she twisted

from side to side. Foxx could tell that he was building too quickly. He grasped Vida's warm-fleshed hips
and lifted her from the dresser, carried her across the
room and fell with her to the bed.

He lay above her now, her legs still resting on his
shoulders, her back arched to bring her buttocks high.
Her hips rose in rhythm with Foxx's as he stroked,
and bit by bit he speeded up the tempo of his thrusts,
driving into her faster and deeper.

Vida's head rolled from side to side on the pillow.
Her eyes were squeezed tightly shut; she was grasp-
ing her full lower lip with her gleaming white teeth.
A few strands of red hair had escaped from their
anchoring pins and floated in tendrils across her face.
Foxx sensed that she was almost ready from the trem-
ors that swept over her body. He stopped holding
back and plunged again and again, enveloping himself in her slick hot depths.

A moan grew deep in Vida's throat. Foxx plunged
and held his body hard against her as she began to
tremble and her moans grew louder, as she strained
to pull him into her still more deeply. He waited
until he felt the quick quivers of Vida's orgasm begin,
and resumed his stroking, slower now, more deliberate, until her hips twisted and she cried, her screams
of painful pleasure loud in his ear.

Then Foxx let go, and his body joined Vida's in
trembling fulfillment as he jetted and drained. Slowly
the ecstasy faded in dying spasms and he let himself
relax on Vida's still-quivering body, and they lay
quiet and spent.

Dusk had crept into the room during their fren-
zied lovemaking without either of them being aware
of it. Vida stirred first. She tried to move her legs,

still trapped under Foxx's chest, and her movement roused him. He raised his shoulders and rolled first to one side, then to the other, and helped her to pull her legs straight. He was still within her, lax now and soft, but when he started to move away, she clasped her arms around him and held him to her.

"No. Not yet, Foxx. We can take our time. Dinner will wait, and I'm just too comfortable right now to move."

He asked lazily, "What about that bath we were going to have?"

"Oh, my God!" Vida gasped. "The tub! I started filling it and forgot to turn the water off!"

Foxx rolled away from her; she sprang up and hurried into the bathroom. In a moment she called, "It's all right. I got here just in time. Come on in whenever you're ready."

When Foxx went into the bathroom, Vida was bending over the brimming tub. Her back was to him, her arms elbow-deep in the water as she groped for the drain to lower the water level.

Her breasts swayed gently as she moved her hands, feeling for the stopper, their tips still protruding from the pink rosettes surrounding them. Below the deep valley of her buttocks Foxx saw the lips of her moist cleft glistening, bright pink and still swollen from their lovemaking, framed invitingly between the fringes of her dark red pubic brush.

Foxx had begun an erection at the first glimpse of Vida in her crouched position over the tub. He stepped up behind her, his bare feet silent on the tiled floor, and guided himself into her. He grasped Vida's hips and pulled her buttocks firmly against him while he waited to become fully hard.

Vida tensed with surprise when she felt him go in. Then she looked over her shoulder at Foxx and said, "You must be a mindreader, Foxx. If you aren't, how did you know I like it in this position, too?"

"Bent over that way, you just seemed to be inviting me."

"Maybe I was, without knowing it." She lifted her hands from the water and grasped the side of the tub. "You'll have to hurry to keep up with me, though. I always finish faster this way."

Completely hard now, Foxx began thrusting. He bent forward to take Vida's dangling breasts in his big hands and to squeeze and caress them. She started to quiver almost at once.

Foxx speeded up, driving himself to meet her timing. Her hips began twisting, her muscles tightened, her breath rasped in deep, gusty sighs from her throat as he pounded home each stroke.

When Vida's back arched suddenly and the cries of her final spasm began, Foxx drove himself harder. He jetted soon after Vida reached her orgasmic peak, and her body began to relax. He held her to his hips as he drained, and supported her limp body a moment longer, until she motioned toward the tub, then helped her in and stretched out beside her.

For a half hour or more they lay suspended in the warm water, their arms cradling one another in a gentle embrace, punctuated by soft kisses. Then Vida reached for the soap, and as the water cooled they luxuriated in the feel of warm flesh slick with soap under their hands, behaving, as Vida pointed out happily, more like children than grown-ups.

"Except I don't feel much like a child, when you

squeeze on me the way you're doing right now," Foxx replied. "Besides, my stomach's beginning to remind me it's empty."

"We'll have dinner, then. And go to my flat afterward. If we came back here, where a C&K call-boy can find you, I wouldn't have you to myself the rest of the night. And that, Foxx, is what I firmly intend to do."

CHAPTER 3

Sunrise was an hour old when Foxx walked into the Cosmopolitan Hotel. The sleepy atmosphere of early morning hung over the usually-busy lobby. Its terrazzo floor was still damp from the mopping that the day porter was just finishing; the porter, Foxx, and the heavy-eyed night desk-clerk had the cavernous lobby to themselves. The desk-clerk called to him before he reached the staircase, and Foxx changed his course in response to the man's call. The clerk pulled a slip of paper from Foxx's box and handed it across the desk.

"Mr. Flaherty asked me to be sure and give you this the minute you got in," the clerk said, handing Foxx the slip.

"What time was Flaherty here?"

"Must've been about one o'clock. He seemed to be a little bit put out because you weren't here."

Reading the scribbled note on the slip, Foxx nodded. "Jim does get a mite impatient, Fred. I guess

you've noticed that, all the times he's been here looking for me. Many thanks. I'll take care of this right
away."

Foxx took his time shaving, then after putting on
a fresh collar and changing boots, he checked his
travel kit. A midnight summons from Flaherty meant
only one thing. Somewhere along the wide-stretched
rails of the California and Kansas Railroad, there was
a problem that needed immediate attention.

Though the big Railroad Regulator clock on the
wall of Jim Flaherty's office showed it to be just past
six, the superintendent of the C&K's Police Division
was waiting when Foxx walked in.

"What'd you do, Foxx?" Flaherty asked. "Start out
tomcatting the minute you stepped off the ferry last
night?"

Foxx fished a stogie out of his pocket and lighted
it before answering. He said mildly, "If I didn't go
when the going was good, I'd never get any time to
myself, Jim."

Eyeing the stogie sourly, Flaherty motioned Foxx
to a chair. He got up and opened a window behind
his desk to allow the smoke from the stubby, twisted
cigar to float out and lose itself in the fog that still
hung low over the peninsula.

"If I thought it'd do any good, I'd keep you in
decent cigars myself," he told Foxx. "Anything'd be
better than those damn ropes you favor."

"Now, Jim, you didn't haul me in here at this time
of day to talk about cigars and tomcatting," Foxx
said. "And you wouldn't've come looking for me last
night if it wasn't something pretty serious. What kind
of trouble have we got now, and whereabouts?"

"Where's easier to answer than what kind." Flaherty picked up the telegrapher's scrawled pink flimsy that lay on top of the pile of papers in the center of his desk. "Kansas."

"Eastern Division, or Western?"

"Eastern. Or maybe Western, for all I can tell from this wire I got from Williams, at Courtland."

Foxx rubbed his chin thoughtfully. "That's where we're thin on manpower, too. I'm still looking for the right man to put at Courtland. But how come you don't know to a tee, Jim?"

"Because Williams didn't say exactly where, damn it!" Flaherty snapped. He shook his head. "It's at the railhead of that new spur we're pushing southwest from the Courtland division point. And if I didn't think it was bad, I wouldn't have gone out looking for you last night."

Foxx frowned. "We've got so damned many spurs building right now that I can't keep all of 'em in mind that easy." He got up and walked over to the C&K system map that covered most of the wall behind Flaherty's desk.

Flaherty joined him and put a finger on the map at the Courtland division point, near the center of the state and just below its northern border. From Courtland, a penciled line ran in a sweeping southwesterly curve almost to the southwest corner where it continued in a series of dots across the narrow strip of Indian Territory that separated Kansas and the Texas Panhandle.

"I'm not sure exactly how far the spur's been pushed by now," Flaherty told Foxx. "It's supposed to go through this little corner of the Indian Nation and into Texas, to a little cowtown in the Panhandle. Amarillo, the place is called."

Foxx nodded. "I know just about where it is. Been a while since I was there, and there wasn't much to it but prairie. Why in hell do we need a spur going to a place like that?"

"Because the country all around it is turning into cattle range, Foxx. Big ranches are jumping up like mushrooms."

Foxx nodded slowly. "I can see that. Flat country, pretty fair grassland, most of it. C&K stands to handle a lot of cars as the ranches grow, I'd guess."

"There's more to it than that. The country that spur's going through in western Kansas is having a land boom, too. Not cattle up there, but wheat."

"Wheat's a good money crop, from what I've heard. Farmers ain't much different from most folks—they like cash, too."

"Seems the whole country wants to move west, Foxx. On top of everything else, Old Cyrus Holliday's been sending recruiters to Europe, and they're bringing farmers over from there by the shipload to settle along that damned little jerkwater line he's promoting."

"You're talking about the Atchison and Topeka?"

"What else? Only don't forget, it's the Atchison, Topeka and Santa Fe, now. They've already pushed iron through Kansas and halfway across Colorado, and Caleb's getting worried. He wants the C&K into Texas before the Holliday line starts laying track to the south, too."

"Hell, Jim, that'll be a long time off. Caleb don't need to worry now. That Atchison and Topeka ain't going to be much but a feeder line for a while."

"You're overlooking the Kansas Pacific, Foxx. They're about halfway across Kansas now, and sur-

veying to the southeast as fast as their crews can
move their transits."

"All right, you've answered my question about the
spur, Jim. Except for telling me what the trouble is."

Flaherty went back to his desk and picked up the
flimsy again. Foxx settled down in his chair. Flaherty
said, "The trouble's gold."

Foxx almost lost his stogie when his jaw dropped
in amazement. He grabbed the twisted cigar before it
hit the floor, and then asked, "Gold?"

"That's right. Work's been stopped on the spur because a bunch of prospectors have filed claims all over
the land it's being built on."

"Now, damn it, Jim, there just ain't any gold in
Kansas!"

Flaherty nodded in agreement. "There never has
been any that I've heard of. It's a couple of hundred
miles too far east to be in gold-mining country. But
that's what Williams says in his wire."

"Gold!" Foxx repeated incredulously. "Jim, that
fellow in Courtland's got to be funning you. Why,
that's where the old Santa Fe Trail ran, years ago.
If there'd been any gold within a hundred miles of
that trail, somebody'd have found it, for sure."

"At this time of day, Foxx, the last thing I need
is a history lesson," Flaherty snapped testily. "It just
happens that I've heard about the Santa Fe Trail
before. But Williams' wire is the only thing I've got
to go by, and if he says gold's been discovered in
Kansas, and prospectors are blocking construction of
that spur, I can't sit on my ass here in San Francisco
and tell him he's wrong."

"So you're going to send me traipsing back to Kansas to tell him for you," Foxx said. He tossed the

butt of his stogie into the spittoon at the corner of
Flaherty's desk. "Seems to me it's a job for the construction super, Jim. It's their business to keep new
trackage pushing ahead on schedule."

"Any other time, I'd agree with you. This is a little
bit more than a construction tie-up, though. I gathered from what Williams said in his wire that a shooting war's just about to break out between the homesteaders who've settled around the railhead and the
gold prospectors."

"So we're expected to get the fracas settled?"

"That's about the size of it," Flaherty nodded. "Any
time there's that kind of trouble, Caleb passes it on
to us. And I can't afford to send just anybody back
there."

Foxx grinned. "I guess I oughta take that as a kind
of left-handed compliment."

"Take it any way you like. Just get back there and
settle whatever mess you find as fast as you can
move."

"Don't get all roiled up, Jim." Foxx stood up.
"I'll catch this morning's nine o'clock mail train and
be in Courtland about day after tomorrow."

"And be sure to send me a message just as soon
as you've found out about that gold strike," Flaherty
told him. "The C&K's got a lot of state subsidy-grant
land along our Kansas trackage, and if there's any
gold there, Caleb wants to send some men to do a
little prospecting of our own."

"Sure. But I'll buy you the biggest steak in San
Francisco when I get back if there's any gold along
that spur. The only way I'm going to believe in a
gold strike in Kansas is to see it with my own two
eyes."

Leaning back on the oilcloth-cushioned bench that ran along the bay of the caboose, Foxx tried to find a soft-spot as he looked out at the rolling country through which the work train was chuffing. He rubbed his cheek. The scab left by Annie Yeager's fingernails was peeling off, and the long red streak was itching constantly.

Progress had been slow since pulling out of Courtland shortly before daybreak. The rails of the new spur hadn't carried enough traffic to be bedded down in the ballast, and the wheels found more jolts than smooth spots. Cutting out a half-dozen boxcars loaded with military supplies at Fort Hays had delayed the train an hour as it crept to and fro on a freshly laid siding, and the afternoon was getting far along.

Adding to Foxx's discomfort was the feeling of frustration he'd been carrying since his conversation with the division superintendent at Courtland. Williams, he'd learned after arriving at the division point shortly before midnight, hadn't made any preparations to get Foxx to his destination. In fact, the division superintendent hadn't seemed to know much of anything about the gold rush that was blocking construction of the new spur.

"That's the construction supe's job," he'd said curtly. "I don't tell him how to run his crews; he doesn't tell me how to operate my division."

"All right, where's the construction super, then?" Foxx had asked.

"He's at the terminal in Kansas City, waiting for that mess down at Sherman to get cleared up so his crew can get to work again."

"Sherman's the place where they've found the gold?"

"Of course. Not right at Sherman, someplace between the railhead and the town."

"How big a town is Sherman?"

"Well, now, I never did take time to go down there and count noses. It's not much of a town, I understand. Five hundred or so people there, I'd guess."

"What about the word we got at the head office that there's trouble building up between the homesteaders around town and the prospectors?"

"I suppose it's true. Sherman's not a right new town. I understand settlement started right after the war. Probably a bunch of veterans, like most new towns hereabouts."

"And some of 'em would figure that the fastest way to settle a fuss is with a gun," Foxx nodded. "That's the way they learned how to do it."

"If you're concerned about our men down at railhead, they've got guns, and C&K property'll be protected," Williams told Foxx stiffly.

"What's the latest word from down that way?" Foxx asked.

"There's not any late word. The telegraph crew ran short of wire, so the construction super pulled them off. He's kept a skeleton crew at railhead, but the only news we get is from the men on the supply accommodation we send down once a week."

"And you haven't been down to take a look yourself?"

"I told you, Mr. Foxx, that's not my job. I've got this division to keep running on time."

"How about this gold? Have you seen any of it?"

"No. But some of the snipes and zebras down at railhead have seen it," the division superintendent said firmly. "Mostly big nuggets, they tell me. About half the size of a man's little finger, some of them. Smaller ones, too, but all of it's real gold. They've put a lot of it to the acid test, and it proved out every test they made."

"Did you ever hear of a gold strike being made in that part of the country before?" Foxx had asked.

Williams had shaken his head thoughtfully. "No. But I guess what they say is true, Mr. Foxx. Gold's where you find it, no matter where that might be."

"Yes. That's what they say, all right. But I still want to look at it myself before I'm satisfied it's real."

Sitting in the caboose bay, Foxx had a clear view of the entire train and a good stretch of the tracks in front of the locomotive. A sharp staccato of toots from the whistle drew his attention. He looked ahead, saw the ground descending, the rails themselves lost to view as they dropped into a wide, shallow valley. Then, when the train dropped over the hump and started downslope, the fresh timbers of a new bridge showed against the shimmering blue-green water of a river.

On the bank, lapped by the stream's slow current, a rock formation stood—three round boulders nested together, rising like curved steps. They would have been overlooked or ignored in areas where rocks were plentiful, but here where boulders of any kind or size were rare, the three massive sand-hued stones were a dominant element in an essentially flat landscape.

Foxx frowned. He'd recognized the formation at first glance, and it aroused memories long dormant and purposely forgotten. It was beside those boulders on the bank of the Smoky Hill River where he'd been given his adult name, a formal adoption into the Kotsoteka Comanche tribe during the sixth winter of his captivity by the Indians.

Although Foxx had purposely shut out of his memories those years when he'd been an alien in a culture not his own, forced to live with the warrior who'd discovered him, there were some memories that he could not force out of his mind.

One of those was of the final desperate moments of the Comanche attack on the wagon carrying the Foxx family west along the Santa Fe Trail. The family was small, Foxx and his parents, and the lone wagon an inviting target for any marauding band that might spot it.

His father had stood off the Comanches for only a short while. Foxx remembered him, an arrow-shaft through his shoulder, reloading the pistol his mother had been using. Then, as the Indian ponies began closing in, Foxx's mother had thrust him into a corner of the wagon and spread a blanket over him, with a harsh command to keep still and stay silent.

Then there had been shots and guttural yells and the wagon had shaken for a few minutes, and after that, silence. When Foxx heard noises again, it was men's voices talking in a language strange to him, and sounds of ripping and crashing. Then there had come the moment when the blanket under which the six-year-old Foxx had been crouching was ripped away and he found himself staring into a pair of obsidian eyes set in a brown-painted face.

"*Quasac!*" the man had called to his companions. "*Quasac!*"

Later, when he'd learned to understand and speak the Comanche tongue, Foxx had learned this was to be his name, and still later he'd learned that the name meant "Boy Under Blanket," or "Boy Covered with Blanket."

It was a name to which he'd answered for six years. During those years, Foxx had learned more than the Comanche tongue. He'd learned the ways of the Kotsoteka Comanche tribe, and his tutors had been mercilessly demanding. He was already past the age when Comanche youths began to learn to manage a horse, and on the farm Foxx's only riding had been done on a tired and gentle plow horse. The half-broken mustangs of the Kotsotekas might have been an entirely different breed of animal from plodding Old Ben. They were small and wiry and seemed to know when whoever was on their back was a novice or afraid.

Each time Foxx failed to execute the horseback maneuvers that Comanche boys his age had already mastered, each time a mustang threw him, Foxx's foster-father cuffed him with a stone-hard hand. He soon realized that he was not being singled out for punishment because he was white and adopted; the same treatment was administered to the young Comanches by their fathers, or by the warriors chosen to tutor them in the skills of riding, hunting, and fighting. And these lessons began at once, too.

Once he'd discovered that he was being taught the same skills in the same ways that his young companions were, Foxx set his teeth and buckled down to absorb his lessons.

He almost caught up with his contemporaries. By the time Foxx was ten, he was joining the other youths in stealing food from the camp's cooking pots, in sneaking out at night to cut horses from the tribe's herd and go on wild gallops across the moonlit prairie. He'd been given a small bow, and learned to shoot birds with cleft arrows, to shoot rabbits with flint-tipped shafts, to stalk a single bird or rabbit for a full day if necessary in order to bring it down.

As he grew older, Foxx joined in the games of mock kidnapping of young girls from the tribe's own tepees, the imitative pastime of setting up a camp where youngsters formed their own tribes and families. There were games of rescue and games of hiding, all of them designed to teach the youths the war and hunting skills they would require as adult warriors.

Memories of his own early life did not quite fade, but were put aside by Foxx in the interest of surviving the rigid Comanche training he was getting. He almost forgot his name, and did forget his age; in later years Foxx was never quite sure whether he'd been five years old or six when his captivity began. Time with the Comanches was not measured by years, but by seasons, and since the seasons varied in length, the white man's method of measuring time by the hands of a clock or by dates on a calendar slid from Foxx's memory, just as did the habits of the Comanches in later years, after Foxx had rejoined his own people.

Seeing the three boulders on the bank of the Smoky Hill River had brought back vividly to Foxx the day when he was told the time had come for him to receive his own adult name. It was the time at which by Comanche standards he had achieved manhood.

His foster father, Ehkemurawa—Red Crooked Nose —had taken Foxx aside and given him the news. "It is time for your naming, my son," the Comanche said. "You are one of The People now."

As was proper for a youth still bearing his baby name, Foxx had stood in respectful silence.

Ehkemurawa continued, "You will go to Tawyawp, who has fought beside me in many battles, and he will talk of this thing to you. He has been watching you closely, and has chosen the name you will be given when we make our winter camp at the River of Smoking Mountains."

Ehkemurawa had not waited for Foxx to agree, or to comment, but had turned and walked away. A command from a Comanche warrior of the stature of Red Crooked Nose was automatically obeyed by any member of the tribe except another warrior of equal standing. In the ways of The People, only equals argued or discussed points of disagreement.

When Foxx went to Tawyawp, the veteran warrior had received him with the gravity that suited the occasion. It was the way of the Comanches for a boy's father to ask one of the tribe's great fighters or one of the medicine chiefs to select a name suitable for his son, and the request was an honor to all three: the one requesting the naming, the one bestowing the name, and the one receiving it.

Tawyawp ordered the women out of his family's tepee and told Foxx to sit down. "I will tell you first why I have chosen the name I will give you," he said. "You are not of our skin, but you have earned a place among The People by learning our ways. You have a skill with horses that equals that of young men born to us. So your name will be Thwaski, White Horse."

"Thank you, my father's friend," Foxx replied. "Is the name mine now, or must I wait to speak it?"

Foxx had known the answer, but by custom the

question had to be asked. Foxx knew that he must
carry the new name as a known but not discussed
matter until he had earned the right to have it announced to the tribe by a deed performed during a
hunt or a fight.

"Kiyou will give you the name when we make winter camp, but you will not bear it until you have
counted coup on an enemy or made a good kill in
a hunt," Tawyawp replied. "Until then, it is only
yours to know."

A month or so later in the tepee of the medicine
chief, Kiyou, pitched as always between the three
sand-colored boulders on the bank of the Smoky Hill
River, Foxx had received his adult name in the presence of Ehkemurawa and Tawyawp. All three of
the men were dressed in full ceremonial regalia, elk-
hide robes painted with their exploits in battle and
hunting, eagle-feather headdresses, and embroidered
moccasins. Their faces were painted as though they
were going into battle.

For a day and a night the medicine chief had kept
Foxx outside the tepee without food or water and
wearing only a loin cloth, so that his body would be
purified. Kiyou had lighted the ceremonial pipe with
a coal from the small fire in the center of the tepee,
and had blown the six puffs of smoke: to the sky,
the earth, and the four points of the compass. Then
he had passed the pipe to Ehkemurawa, who had
made the six puffs in turn and handed the pipe to
Tawyawp.

After the pipe was laid aside, Kiyou had intoned
a prayer and risen to his feet. Taking Foxx by the
hand, Kiyou led him outside with the others following. The medicine chief had taken the spear that

stood outside the tepee and held it erect in front of him. Foxx stood facing him, the rising sun warm on his bare torso, forcing himself to keep his eyes open in spite of the red glare that stung them.

Kiyou intoned another prayer, a very brief one, then turned to address the sun. "O Sun, you see this man." Bowing his head, Kiyou said, "O Earth, you hold this man." Raising his head, "O Sky, you cover this man." Then, fixing his eyes on Foxx, Kiyou had said, "O man, here with the sun and earth and sky to witness, I give you the name Thwaski."

Looking at the three massive boulders, Foxx could almost see himself as a youth, standing with the sun's glare in his face. As events developed, he was to bear the name only a short time. It had been announced officially just a few months before he'd been returned to white civilization by a band of buffalo hunters who'd surprised the Comanche hunters with Foxx. The first volley of shots from the heavy Sharps .50s carried by the white men had killed two of Foxx's companions. One of the men killed was Ehkemurawa.

By the time the work train had crossed the bridge and the three boulders were out of sight, Foxx had shut out the memory and was back in his present world again.

CHAPTER 4

Foxx swung off the caboose while the work train was still creaking to a stop. Carrying his valise, he walked toward the locomotive, the soles of his Nocona-made cavalry-heel boots crunching on the loose gravel that spilled out along the freshly laid roadbed.

Two boxcars, the board sides of one of them pierced with small windows, stood on the spur just ahead of the locomotive. In front of the boxcars a handcar had been placed sidewise across the track, a few yards back from the last pair of rails. Four men lounged on the handcar's platform; their shapeless clothes and grimy hands marked them as belonging to the track-laying crew. Two rifles and two double-barreled ten-gauge shotguns lay beside them on the pumper, within easy reach.

Stopping at the handcar, Foxx glanced ahead. Where the rails ended, a low barricade of crisscrossed ties had been erected on the fresh gravel that extended a few feet past the raw railends. On the other side of the ties the ground was clear for perhaps fifty yards, where a low dirt embankment had been shoveled up. The bank stretched across the front line of the diggings, and Foxx could see three or four men sitting behind it. He wondered whether it had been erected by the prospectors to keep the C&K men out, or by the track crew to mark a deadline between the diggings and the railhead.

From the earthworks on, the ground looked like a freshly harrowed farm field. The area was dotted by widely spaced tents, and a few—a very few—wooden houses, little more than huts. There were still fewer of the low-humped rises that marked the location of sod houses. Every inch of earth that Foxx could see had been spaded and turned, and everywhere mounds of dark, fresh dirt rose, some of them waist-high.

It looked as though a tribe of giant gophers had invaded the place, Foxx thought. Dirt was flying in a few spots where digging was going on, and there were perhaps a dozen men wandering around over the broken soil, among the tents.

Foxx estimated that the area of the diggings extended for at least a mile to the point where a huddle of buildings rose, and stretched as far as he could see on both sides. With the just-recalled memories of his early youth still fresh in his mind, Foxx now remembered something further he'd learned then: on the flat prairie a man on foot could see plainly for about three miles, a man on horseback almost seven.

All four of the men on the handcar had been examining Foxx without bothering to hide their curiosity. Now one of them asked, "You looking for somebody, mister? Because there ain't nobody but C&K men supposed to be around here."

"My name's Foxx. C&K police, detective division. Where's your foreman?"

"Grogan? Pounding his ear in the bunkhouse car, I guess." The man jerked a thumb over his shoulder.

Foxx nodded his thanks and walked back to the door of the bunkhouse car. He levered himself up the strap-step into the car. The interior was dark. He stood in the doorway until his eyes adjusted to the dimness. A double row of a half-dozen cots each lined the car's walls at one end; the other end contained a table and shelves and a sheet-iron stove. Only three of the dozen cots were occupied, the men in them sleeping. The sour smell of unwashed clothes and sweaty bodies was heavy in the car.

"Which one of you is Grogan?" Foxx asked.

"That's me," one of them said. "What the hell you want?"

"Information."

"Listen here, if you're one of them newspaper fellows, you might as well hightail back where you come from. I got orders not to talk to you guys or let you come on railroad property."

"My name's Foxx. C&K detective division."

"Well, why didn't you say so right off?" Grogan sat up on the side of the cot and looked at Foxx blearily. "I took the night-watch last night. Give me a minute to wake up."

Foxx lighted a stogie while the foreman rubbed sleep out of his eyes. Grogan had been sleeping fully dressed, even to his heavy brogans. He stood up and indicated that they were to go outside. When he saw the work train on the tracks behind the boxcars, the foreman shook his head.

"I didn't even hear the no-bill come in," he told Foxx. "You been here long?"

"Just a few minutes."

Grogan nodded. Taking a step away from Foxx, he unbuttoned his fly and started urinating on the ground.

Foxx was getting impatient. He said, "I guess you can talk and piss at the same time?"

"Sure," Grogan replied cheerfully. "What d'you wanta know?"

"That town up ahead, it'd be Sherman?"

"Yep. What there is left of it. They say there's been a lot of digging in the streets and around the houses. I ain't been there since the trouble started."

"What kind of trouble?"

"About what you'd expect. Them that don't believe it's a real goldfield don't want the town dug up. The prospectors don't want to stop digging. A few fights is all it amounts to, from what I can figure out." Grogan was buttoning his fly.

Foxx asked him, "You had any trouble along the tracks out here?"

Grogan pointed to the guards on the handcar, and the men behind the dirt embankment. "Not since we started standing watches. Them prospector sons of bitches have found out it ain't safe to mess with our right of way."

"Anybody taken a shot at your men?" Foxx asked.

"There was some serious shooting, right at first, but shit! All my men and me, we went through the war, on one side or the other. We don't spook easy. I guess most of them fellows out there are about like us. Ever since we figured things out, we've just been standing pat. Us and them, too."

"You think there's a chance the shooting's going to start again?"

"Who the hell knows? Like I said, none of us been into town since all this dustup started." Grogan scratched into his three-day growth of beard. "We got orders to stay clear of whatever happens off the right of way. But if anybody starts digging on railroad land, anywheres close to the tracks, we got orders to stop 'em."

"That sounds all right to me," Foxx said. Then he cautioned, "Just don't let any of your men get trigger-happy."

Grogan snorted. "Not much chance of that Mr.— Foxx, was it?" Foxx nodded, and the foreman asked curiously, "Just where in hell do you fit into this? Not that it's any of my business, I guess, but I'd sure like to know. You the boss now?"

"If any trouble breaks out, I'd expect you and your men to do what I tell you to. I won't be giving you orders about anything else, though."

"That sounds fair enough," Grogan agreed. "I guess a man in your kind of job must know how to handle things in a showdown."

"If it comes to a showdown, I'll be on hand," Foxx told him. "I wouldn't like to see that happen, though. The C&K's got enough problems without taking on a whole damn town."

"Hell, none of the folks in town's mad at us. Them prospectors, now, that's something else again. They want digging rights on our trackage."

"I won't worry, Grogan, as long as you and your men are on guard." Foxx was changing his earlier opinion of the foreman. He said, "You've been here since this gold rush started, haven't you?"

"I sure as hell have."

"How much gold have you seen since all this digging's been going on?"

"Some. Not a big lot."

"You're sure it's gold? Not pyrites or something else that looks like gold?"

"Oh, it's real gold, all right. They tested it with acid and everything." Grogan grinned. "Sorta made me feel like going out and doing some digging myself. Most of my crew did go. I had twenty men before the gold fever hit. Now I got six."

"Well, I've still got to see some of that gold for myself before I'll believe it," Foxx said.

"You'll have to go into Sherman for that."

"I figured I would. That being the case, I might as well get started. There's not a lot I can do out here."

Foxx picked up his valise and walked around the barricade into the clear area between the railhead and the diggings. The men behind the dirt embankment stood up and watched as he crossed the clear space. He noticed that they were all holding rifles and wore pistol belts. Stopping a polite distance from them, Foxx said, "You men mind if I walk on past you, into town?"

"That depends on who you are and what you're going to town for," one of them replied.

"My name's Foxx. I work for the C&K."

"Hell, we figured that out when we seen you over there talking to Grogan. Thing we're interested in is what business you got in Sherman."

"Nothing special. I just want to take a look at the place."

"Why? Sherman's not much different to towns like you've seen before."

"I didn't figure it would be. Except the C&K's trying to get this spur track pushed in there and beyond, and you men seem to be blocking the way."

"And we'll stay right here till Ben Mercer tells us to move. He'll be here in a minute; one of the boys has gone after him."

"Who's Mercer?" Foxx asked. "Your boss?"

"We got no bosses here. Ben made the first strike, him and his partner. I guess if we had a mayor in the diggings, it'd be Ben. I imagine he'll be curious why you headed for town the minute you hopped off your train."

"Maybe if I get a closer look at the place, my bosses would decide to go around Sherman instead of through it."

"You really expect us to fall for that?" the man sneered. "It's more likely your damn railroad's getting ready to help them sodbusters get rid of us. That's what the C&K and the town'd both like to do."

"No. You men have got things figured all wrong. If there's a real goldfield here, the C&K's going to make a pot of money hauling machinery in and gold ore out."

"That stands to reason, Zeb," one of the other men said.

Foxx pressed the slight advantage he sensed he'd gained. He said, "I won't lie to you men. The C&K's on its own side first of all. We don't care whose freight we're hauling, whether it's wheat or gold or cattle, as long as it makes money for us."

"That sounds like a straight answer if I ever heard one," Zeb admitted. "You know—"

Before he could finish, the man who'd gone after Ben Mercer returned, accompanied by a stocky, florid-faced individual who Foxx assumed was the prospectors' unofficial spokesman.

Mercer looked at Foxx through squinted eyes. "Chesty told me what was going on," he said. "Told me you're talking for the railroad, now. I sure as hell hope you make more sense than the other C&K men we've had jawing at us."

"Now, wait a minute," Foxx said. "I didn't come here to make you men no promises, or work any deals. All I can tell you is what I just told your friend here." He repeated what he'd said about the type of freight hauled making no difference to the railroad.

"Sounds to me like he's talking sense, Ben," Zeb volunteered when Foxx had finished. "How does it strike you?"

"I'd wanta hear him talk some more," Mercer replied.

Foxx said, "Oh, there's more to it than that. The government gives the C&K a section of land along the right of way for every mile of track we lay. Now, I guess you know a section's not much of a wheat farm, but there can sure be a lot of gold on six hundred and forty acres. What makes you think the railroad's not interested in finding out whether there's gold on some of that land?"

"You make it sound like the damn railroad's on our side," Mercer said suspiciously.

"Meaning you don't feel right about the C&K?"

"Listen, Foxx," Mercer went on, "your damned railroad give us a lot of trouble, right at first. And if we make any strikes on what you claim is railroad land, we might have more trouble. Because I'll tell you this. We're after gold, and wherever it's in the ground, we're going to get it out."

"Nobody in his right mind'd blame you for feeling that way," Foxx answered. "But that's neither here nor there, Mercer. All I'm interested in right now is going in to take a look at Sherman."

"I don't see where a lone man can hurt us," Mercer told the other prospectors. "We got to straighten things out with the sodbusters sooner or later. He might be able to help do it."

Zeb looked at the other guards, who nodded agreement. He said to Mercer, "That's about how we saw it." Then, to Foxx, he added, "Just don't give none of us trouble, and you won't get into none."

"Trouble's the last thing I'm after," Foxx assured them. He looked at Mercer. "If you're going back toward town, maybe I can walk along with you. These men said you and your partner found the first gold here. That's a story I'd kinda like to hear."

"Sure. Come along," Mercer agreed.

Foxx and Mercer walked together toward the town. They picked their way through the pockmarkings of holes that had been started and abandoned, around piles of dirt and prospectors' tents and bedrolls spread on the bare ground. Foxx, in his city suit and homburg, drew a succession of curious glances from those who greeted Mercer.

Foxx waited until he felt Mercer was accustomed to his company before asking, "How'd you and your partner happen to make this strike, anyhow? Far as

I can recall, nobody's ever found gold in Kansas before."

"Listen, we was the most took back of anybody," Mercer grinned. "Me and Red come here to homestead, see? And before we filed a homestead claim, we figured this is pretty dry country, so we better see if we couldn't find a place where we'd be sure to have water. So, we hired a water witch."

"Plenty of folks say there is such things," Foxx said noncommittally.

"Sure. Funny thing, our water witch is a whore in town, here. Girl name of Daisy, works in the house back of the saloon. It was her picked the place, a little ways past an old buffalo wallow. We dug where her forked stick pointed to, and damned if we didn't bring up four of the prettiest gold nuggets you ever seen about the second shovelful of dirt we turned."

"How'd you know it was gold?"

"Why, the shovel cut right into one of them nuggets. I had to twist and work to get it off, and when I looked at it to see what kind of rock was so soft, there was that yellow gold shining up at me."

"So you kept on digging and found some more?" Foxx asked.

"You're damn right we did! And we found more, too. Not just where we'd dug before, but all around there."

Foxx waved a hand to encompass the diggings. "And that's how all this started?"

"Yep. Man never knows, does he?"

"I reckon not." Foxx frowned. "I'd guess you kept that first nugget for a souvenir?"

"Wouldn't you have? I got it right here in my poke."

Mercer took out a buckskin bag. Foxx could see at a glance that it wasn't very well-filled. The prospector fumbled with his fingers in the little sack and drew out a twisted chunk that Foxx assumed was the nugget. He handed it over.

Foxx hefted the nugget; it felt heavy and substantial enough to be gold. When he looked at it closely, he saw the gash cut by the shovel, and in its vee the soft yellow sheen that Mercer had described. As far as Foxx could tell, the object he held was indeed a nugget of almost pure gold. He handed it back to Mercer.

"It sure looks good. You tested it, I guess?"

"Damn right, I did! Tested the other ones that was in the same shovelful, and I'd bet everybody else that's dug up any has tested what they've dug, too."

"A lot of the others have found nuggets like this one?" Foxx asked.

For the first time, Mercer acted uncertain. "Well, maybe not a lot. You know how it is, Foxx. There's some that's made strikes and just ain't talking about 'em till all this land mess gets straightened around. But there's been more gold found, I know that."

"Did Daisy witch the claims for the men that made strikes?"

Mercer shook his head. "No. I guess her finding our strike was a fluke. After she tried a few times more and didn't turn up any more gold, or any water either, all of us just give up on her."

"These other strikes, are they all right-close to where you made your first find?" Foxx asked.

"Nossir! Some of them strikes was made half a mile

or more from where me and Red staked our claim."

"Well, it sure looks like you men got a goldfield here," Foxx said. "How many prospectors you figure to've come in here since the word started getting spread around?"

"It'd be hard to tell, Foxx. There's no place close where a man can file a mining claim, so none of us has filed, yet. There was a few of us already here. They was like me and Red, getting ready to file for homesteads."

"You mean nobody's filed on any of these claims at all?"

"Not yet. Hell, the closest place there is to file is at Fort Dodge, and there ain't no stagecoach runs to Sherman. It's two days up and two days back, if you got a horse, which most of us ain't. You go on a mule, it's a day extra each way. Who's going to leave his claim that long?" Mercer shook his head. "Not nobody in his right mind."

"I can see that, if nobody's filed, yet," Foxx agreed.

"We tried to get your damn railroad to sell us tickets to Fort Hays, or to let us ride the work train up to where we'd be able to hoof it to Fort Dodge fast, but they said they couldn't do that."

"Well, whoever told you that was telling the truth. But it sure looks to me like you're running a big risk, not filing."

"Oh, we've got a lawyer in Sherman working on a way for us to file. New man in town, J. Cornelius Abernathy. He's the one advised us to go along the way we are; says he can make sure we won't lose anything by putting off filing."

"If he knows Kansas land law, which I don't, I

guess you're all right, then. But a lawyer can't keep you from losing out to some quick-drawing claim jumper," Foxx said thoughtfully.

"We thought about that, too. After we jawed about it a little bit, we all agreed we'd act just like our claims was filed, and any strangers that come nosing around, we'd keep an eye on 'em and stand together against 'em, if they turned out to be claim jumpers."

"Sheriff couldn't help you out?"

"There ain't no sheriff. Just a town marshal, and he's got nothing to say about what happens outside the town limits. Oh, he said he'd do what he could. But there's only him and one deputy, and they're apt to be out of pocket when they're needed worst. It's worked all right, so far. There's enough of us around now so we can handle our own trouble."

"You never did say how many of you men are working claims around here," Foxx reminded him.

Mercer glanced around the busy diggings. "Oh, close to a hundred, I'd bet. Not counting the folks in town that're digging on their own land, and in the street, some of 'em."

"Well, you might spread the word around that the C&K's not mad at anybody, and won't be as long as you men don't go tearing up our right of way."

"You mean that?"

"You can take my word, Mercer. Like I told you awhile ago, the only thing we're interested in is getting our crew back to work on that spur. The road's not siding with anybody. You prospectors or the homesteaders or anybody else."

"I'll sure pass that along, Foxx. Now, my claim's right off here a little ways, and I got to get back and see how Red's doing. Stop by and say hello on your way back to the tracks."

"Thanks. I just might do that, if it's not too late."

Foxx continued toward town after Mercer veered off at a right angle to the direction in which they'd been walking. When he reached the edge of the diggings, he found another earth embankment between them and the town itself. A horse stood in the clear area between the bank and Sherman's first houses, and beside the horse a man was sitting with his legs folded flat, Comanche-style.

He saw Foxx approaching and rose to his feet. He was exceptionally tall and almost painfully thin. He wore a gunbelt that carried a holstered revolver, and Foxx noticed that there was a rifle in a saddle scabbard on the horse. A nickle-plated star was pinned to his shirt pocket.

"You mind stopping to visit for a minute, friend?" he asked.

"Be glad to." Foxx stopped and set his valise on the ground. He dug a stogie out of his pocket and lighted it. When the thin man said nothing more, he looked pointedly at the badge on his shirt and asked, "Well, what's on your mind, Marshal?"

"No, sir. Ed Parsons is the marshal. I'm his deputy."

"Well, we're in pretty much the same line of work. My name's Foxx. Detective division, C&K Railroad."

"Pleased to make your acquaintance, Mr. Foxx. My name's Edwards. Most folks call me Slim."

Foxx acknowledged the introduction with a nod, but said nothing.

Edwards asked, "You've just come through the diggings from the railhead, I guess?"

"Well, now, I'd have a hell of a time getting to town unless I'd come through the diggings, wouldn't I?"

A thin smile flickered across the tall deputy's lips. "I guess you would, at that."

Foxx waited, but the deputy remained silent, a small frown pulling his brows together. To start the conversation again, Foxx asked, "You're standing guard to keep the prospectors and the townsfolk separated, I suppose?"

Edwards nodded. "The marshal don't want any more trouble between 'em."

"I heard there's some bad feelings there," Foxx nodded. "Well, Slim, if that's all you wanted, I'll be on my way."

For a moment Edwards hesitated, then he asked, "You going to town to see anybody in particular?"

"No. Just looking. Why? Have you closed the town down to the prospectors, or something like that?"

"Not by no means. Hell, Mr. Foxx, they got to be able to go in and buy grub, have a drink, get clothes or tools or whatever. And half of 'em or more has to haul water from the town well. No, Ed just keeps me out here in case some of the folks from town start getting outa line. That's all."

"I see." Foxx glanced at the sun, now just touching the western horizon and beginning to change color from eye-stabbing gold to a rosy pink. "Well, I'd better be getting along. I'd like to have time to have a look around before it gets too dark."

Foxx picked up his valise, gave Slim Edwards a farewell nod, and started walking across the strip of unbroken ground that lay between him and the first shabby houses of Sherman.

CHAPTER 5

Foxx had seen enough expanding towns along the
C&K's tracks to recognize the manner in which Sherman had grown. The process was akin to the growth
of a tree, which adds a fresh layer, a new ring of
wood around its central core with each passing year.

Three layers of settlement showed in the buildings
that made up the little town, and Foxx could iden-
tify each one at a glance. The earliest homesteaders
had managed over the course of years to haul in
enough scarce and expensive lumber to build wooden
houses. These older dwellings and several large business buildings formed Sherman's core. The frame
structures were clustered untidily on both sides of
the somewhat wavering street that ran through the
town.

Most of the settlers that had come in the second
wave still lived in sod houses, but there were a few
hide-shacks visible. The soddies had been built by
cutting blocks of root-laced topsoil and laying them

in rows like bricks, using mud for mortar. The hide-houses were made by driving corner-posts into the ground and nailing green buffalo hides to them to form walls. The inch-thick hides, dried by being stretched flat on the ground and staked along their edges, were sawed into rectangles or squares. A wall made from these panels was almost as rigid and enduring as one made from lumber.

For the most part, the soddies and hide-houses rose in a ragged circle around the older dwellings. The newest arrivals, most of them prospectors, Foxx thought to himself, had put up tents or crude shacks, little more than huts. These formed Sherman's outer perimeter, a straggling line of unevenly spaced temporary shelters between the diggings and the dwellings of the settlers who'd gotten there earlier.

Foxx continued his unhurried stroll until he drew close enough to the center of town to read the signs identifying the three largest of the business buildings. Even without the signs, he would have been able to make a good guess as to the kind of business each of the larger structures housed: livery stable, general store, and saloon.

There were few people on the street, most of them seeming to be in a hurry to attend to some matter of urgent importance before the sun's upper rim dropped out of sight. There were none too intent on their own purposes, though, to inspect Foxx closely as they passed.

A ramshackle wagon, its wide wheels grating on the packed dirt street, was rumbling away from the store as Foxx approached it. There was another wagon and a buggy at the hitch-rail outside the store, flanked by a pair of mules laden with packsaddles. Foxx stepped up to the board sidewalk in front of the store and set his valise at his feet while he lighted a stogie. Two men pushed through the swinging doors of the saloon across the street and headed for the store. Foxx moved aside to let them enter.

He was still standing there, debating whether to ask in the store or in the saloon where he might find a room and a place to eat, when angry voices from inside the store interrupted his deliberation. Stepping up to the door, Foxx looked inside.

In front of the counter that extended toward the back of the store, the two men who'd just gone into the store were standing. Their backs were toward Foxx, their arms raised. Facing them was an overall-clad man, a pistol in his hand, threatening the two new arrivals. Farther down the counter stood two other men. Foxx took one of them to be the store-keeper from the apron he wore, the second man had on a business suit.

"Scum of the earth, that's what you are!" the man holding the pistol was shouting when Foxx looked in. "Dregs from no place, come to tear up what hard-working men has put in their time to build!"

Neither of the two men being threatened by the pistol replied to the angry tirade. They stood frozen, motionless, not even turning their heads to exchange glances.

"Now, hold on, Eb!" the storekeeper said, sidling along the counter to where the three stood. "These fellows didn't give you no cause to jump 'em! Why don't you put that gun away and act halfway sensible?"

"Sensible, my asshole!" the man called Eb snorted over his shoulder. "If we get many more of these

damned prospectors crowding in here, a farmer won't
have no more chance than a snowball in hell to
make hisself a crop! I had my fill of 'em! So has the
rest of us!"

"Listen, mister, it's a free country!" one of the
prospectors said. "If I want to prospect instead of
farming, I got the right!"

"Not when you rip up the land a man's worked
on trying to make a crop! Not when you tear out
what he's planted!"

"Wait a minute!" the second prospector said. "We
ain't turned a shovelful of dirt around here yet!
Damn it, we just got to town less'n an hour ago!"

"That don't matter!" Eb replied. "I had all I can
stand! From now on, I'm shooting prospectors on
sight! Starting with you two!"

Foxx saw that the farmer had worked himself up
to the point of killing. He had no time to reach
the man. Lifting his valise, he lobbed it through the
door. The little suitcase sailed over the raised arms of
the two being held at gunpoint and came down as
Foxx had planned, on Eb's gun-arm. The weight
of the valise knocked the arm down just as Eb's
finger tightened on the trigger. The slug from the
pistol ripped into the floor.

By that time, Foxx had pushed between the two
prospectors and grabbed the revolver. He wrapped
his hand around it to hold the cylinder motionless,
effectively preventing a second shot. Eb struggled,
but Foxx held on. The storekeeper vaulted the counter and clamped his hands on the struggling farmer's forearms. Foxx finally wrested the gun away.

"You men make yourselves scarce," the storekeeper
told the two prospectors. "I guess you came in for

supplies, and I'll be glad to take care of you as soon as this business is cleared up."

"What d'you think?" one of them asked the other.

"Hell, we come a long way to try our luck on this new strike," the second man replied. "I don't aim to let one sorehead sodbuster drive me off."

"All right," his companion nodded. He told the storekeeper, "We'll get outa your way awhile and come back in."

Their heads close together in whispered consultation, the two left the store. Foxx and the storekeeper were still holding the farmer immobilized. Eb sighed, sagged, and admitted defeat.

"All right, Boyd. You can let go of me," he said. "If you're on their side, too, I guess all of us had just as well give up and pull stakes."

"Now, there's no reason for you to feel that way, Eb," the merchant said, releasing the man. "I'm on your side just as much as I am on anybody's."

"Like hell!" Eb said angrily. If you was with us farmers, you wouldn't sell nothing to them damn gold-grubbers!"

"Be reasonable, Eb," the storekeeper urged. "I'm in business to sell to whoever comes in to buy. I can't close my doors to a man just because I don't like what he's doing."

"Boyd, do you know what a bunch of them bastards did to me?" When the storekeeper shook his head, Eb went on bitterly, "You know them peach trees I put in on my back forty last year?"

"I recall you were right proud of them," Boyd replied.

"Lemme tell you about them trees," Eb went on. "I spent a month grubbing out the damn buffalo grass all around where I set 'em out, so's their roots could spread. I hauled water in buckets all last summer to get 'em started. And then what happened? I'll tell you. Three of them damned prospectors showed up day before yesterday and dug up every one of them little trees like they wasn't nothing but weeds! Just to make room for them to dig on my land, looking for gold!"

"Now, that's a shame." Boyd shook his head sympathetically. "But I sure don't know what we can do about it."

"Well, if we don't find a way to do something pretty quick, there's going to be trouble." Eb turned to Foxx and said, "I guess I owe you, mister, for keeping me from shooting that gold-grubber son of a bitch. Don't quite know whether I'm glad or sorry, though." He held out his hand. "But you can give me my gun back. I won't go off half-cocked any more."

Wordlessly, Foxx returned the revolver. The man in the business suit stepped up to join them. He took Eb's arm and led him to one side. Dropping his voice, he said, "With all the work you've put in on your homestead, Eb, you've got a good property there. Now, you understand, I'm not pressing you to do anything you'd regret, but if you do decide you want to leave it, let me know. I'm sure we can work out some kind of deal."

"Thanks, Mr. Ingersoll," Eb nodded. "I was pretty hot when I said what I did. I reckon I'll tough it out awhile longer."

"Whatever you decide to do," Ingersoll nodded. "If you change your mind about staying, though, let me know first."

With a nod and a halfhearted effort at a smile, the farmer left. Boyd turned to Foxx and said, "You acted right quick, mister. Saved a bunch of trouble, too. So far, there hasn't been any killing here, but things are just about ready to bust wide open."

Foxx nodded. "So I see. Well, I didn't mean to butt in, but I hated to see what was about to happen." He picked up his valise. "I'd better be getting along now. I'll see you men around town, I guess, later on."

Without seeming to hurry, but without giving the others a chance to ask questions, Foxx walked out. He hesitated for a moment, then crossed the street to the saloon. He'd always found that in a strange town a chat with a barkeeper and the scraps of conversation overheard at the bar would provide him with more useful information than he'd get by asking a dozen direct questions.

Given the name of the town, Foxx was not surprised to see that Sherman's saloon also had a predictable name, The Union. Its interior offered no surprises, either. As he pushed through the swinging doors, it struck Foxx that the place was a virtual duplicate of a score or more that he'd seen in as many widely scattered frontier towns along the C&K's tracks.

For all its raw, unfinished appearance, the saloon had seen plenty of use. Its wide board floor was scarred and battered. The bar ran halfway along one side of its narrow interior; at the end of the bar, a balcony jutted out, rooms opening onto it. Below the overhang of the balcony, tables covered with faded green felt stood ready for gambling. There were no games in progress, but a shirt-sleeved house man wearing the traditional green eyeshade sat ready to accommodate anyone looking for a game.

Behind the bar, shelves held rows of bottles; a fly-specked mirror was set between them in the center. An aproned barkeeper stood waiting for customers. Bare, unpainted tables filled the narrow area between the bar and the opposite wall. Only one of the tables was occupied, and Foxx recognized the two men who sat at it as the pair who'd fled from the store. They recognized hm as quickly and one of them intercepted him before Foxx reached the bar.

"I don't know who you are, mister," the man said, "but me and my partner sure do thank you for saving our bacon there in the store. That crazy sodbuster was ready to cut us down. What the hell's wrong with folks in this town? They all act like that fellow did?"

"I couldn't answer that," Foxx replied. "I just pulled into town myself. But I got the idea prospectors don't stand very high with the homesteaders hereabouts."

"If any more things like that happen, me and Cam'll most likely absquatulate. There's other places we can go, where folks won't throw down on us the first time they see us."

"Well, if it's supplies you're after, the coast's clear now at the store. But if I was you, I wouldn't let my mouth work faster than my brain until things settle down around here."

"Don't worry. Well, thanks again. We'd like to buy you a drink, if you'd care to join us."

"No offense, but I've got business to tend to. Next

time we run into one another, I'll take you up with thanks."

"Sure." The prospector returned to the table, and after he and his companion had exchanged a few words, the two left the saloon.

Foxx walked up to the bar and set his valise at his feet. The barkeep came up to serve him.

"What's your pleasure, friend?" the man asked.

Foxx studied the bottles on the shelves. Not all of them had labels, and some of those bearing distillery labels had been opened. He spotted a familiar name on an unopened bottle and pointed to it.

"Cyrus Noble suits my taste just right."

"It's a full bottle, friend," the barkeep pointed out after glancing over his shoulder.

"Funny, I noticed that myself." Foxx tossed a half eagle on the bar. "I'll be in town a few days. Suppose you just write my name on the front of it, and set it out for me when I stop in for a drink."

"Be glad to." The barkeep took the bottle off the shelf and rummaged through the till until he found a pencil. "Let's see, I didn't get your name."

"Foxx. With two x's." Foxx watched while the man printed his name on the label, then took a corkscrew from beneath the bar and pulled the cork. When the barkeep set out a glass and poured, Foxx said, "Pour one for yourself, too."

"No, thanks. It ain't that I don't admire your taste in whiskey, but I don't touch the stuff while I'm working." The barkeep hesitated, then said, "But I'll take a cigar instead, if it's all the same to you."

"A smoke or a drink, it's all the same."

While the barkeep selected a cigar from a box on the backbar, Foxx took a stogie from his pocket.

The barkeep turned, holding the cigar he'd chosen. He saw the stogie and struck a match, holding it for Foxx.

"I just finished a smoke myself," he said apologetically. "I guess I'll save this one for later." Foxx nodded. He knew quite well the cigar would go back into the box later, and that the barkeep would pocket its price.

"You say you'll be here awhile," the barkeep said. "In the gold-mining business, are you?"

"No. C&K Railroad." Foxx took a sip of whiskey. "All the gold fever that's hit the town's holding up that spur we're pushing south."

"It's a damn shame, too," the barkeep nodded. "Sherman's been waiting a long time for a railroad line."

"Well, you'll have one, soon as we can get back to work on the right of way."

"I don't guess you can say how long that'll be?"

Foxx shook his head. "I just got here. Soon as I find a place to stay and get a chance to do some talking around town, I might have an idea."

"If you're looking for a place to bunk, I've got a vacant room upstairs," the barkeep offered.

Foxx looked up at the balcony with its row of doors. He said, "No offense, but when I go to bed, I like to sleep. I don't imagine I'd get much rest with the girls taking customers back and forth all night."

"We don't run whores here," the man said. "They've got a shack across the alley in back. And they're on their own. They don't pick up customers in here."

"That makes it different," Foxx nodded. "All right, I'll take your vacant room."

"Number Five," the barkeep said. He went on rapidly, reciting a familiar routine. "Key's in the door. Sheets changed every week regular, clean towels on Wednesday and Saturday. China boy comes in to fill your water pitcher and make up the bed every day. Bathtub down at the end of the hall, but you need to say in advance when you'll want it. Costs a dollar a day. In advance."

"Keep the rest of that half eagle," Foxx said. "Put what's left over the price of the bottle on the room. Let me know when I owe you some more."

"You figuring on—"the barkeep began, then broke off as the batwings clacked and another customer came in. The bartender said to Foxx, "If you're trying to find out what's happening in Sherman, you'll be wanting to do some talking to folks. Here's a real good man for you to start with."

"Evening, Bert," the newcomer nodded, stopping next to Foxx in front of the bar. "I'll have my usual."

"Coming up right away, Frank," the barkeep said. "You might like to get acquainted with Mr. Foxx while I fix you up. He's with the C&K." To Foxx he said, "This here's Frank Morse. He's the local reporter for the newspaper in Hays."

"And the Topeka paper, too," Morse said. He extended his hand to Foxx. "Whatever the railroad does is good for a story, Foxx. What brings you to Sherman?"

"Not anything you'd want to put in your paper right now," Foxx replied.

"If you'd care to tell me, strictly off the record, I won't let a word get into print until you say I can release it," Morse promised.

"That might make a difference," Foxx admitted.

"Tell you what, maybe we could do a little bit of swapping."

Bert put a tall glass on the bar in front of Morse. The newspaperman sampled the drink, looking thoughtfully at Foxx. He took his glass from his lips and said, "A swap never did any harm, I guess."

"I won't guarantee to give you as good value as I'll expect to get," Foxx warned.

"Then, I'll go into it with my eyes open, won't I?" Morse smiled. "If we're going to talk in confidence, we can move to one of the tables where we'll be private."

"Why don't we just do that," Foxx agreed. Newspapermen could be as prolific a source of information as barkeepers.

Foxx sized up Morse as they carried their drinks to a table near the back of the saloon. The reporter was well past middle age; he was tall, but paunchy. His cheeks shone a healthy pink above an untrimmed salt-and-pepper moustache that masked his lips before merging with a well-tended spaded beard. Eyebrows as bushy as the moustache sprouted above twinkling blue eyes.

Morse led the way to an isolated table and they sat down. He asked, "Did you come to Sherman to take charge of the new spur's construction, Foxx?"

"Construction's not my line. I guess you could call me a troubleshooter. That's about as close as you'd get."

Morse frowned thoughtfully. "Are you saying you're going to try to arrange with the prospectors to get a clear right of way through their claims?" He shook his head. "I don't think they'd be very likely to listen to you. Most of them have a full-grown case of gold fever."

"I've just been around here a little while, but I've already found that out," Foxx replied.

"Then you've probably found out that there's bad feeling between the folks who homesteaded here to start farms and the new bunch that have come in after the gold strike."

"It'd be hard to miss noticing it. I was in the store a minute ago when a farmer was ready to shoot a couple of prospectors who'd just come to town. I'd say feelings are running pretty high. Am I right?"

"I'm afraid the only answer I can give you is yes and no. It's not like a grudge that's been building for years, but it's deep enough." Morse sipped his drink and added, "I'm not sure which is worse, though, an old grudge or a fresh new one."

Foxx nodded. "I've seen both kinds, and I can't help but agree with you. Whose side are you on, if you don't object to me asking?"

"All I want to see is a peaceful town. I'm trying not to favor either side. I don't know that my influence is worth much, though. There's not many people take papers here."

"You're the only reporter around, though," Foxx pointed out.

"Yes. But I've been in the business long enough not to overestimate the influence of the printed word."

Foxx nodded. Then he asked, "I've heard a couple of names I'm sorta curious about."

"I suppose I know the names of the folks who've been here awhile. Not the new bunch of prospectors, of course. There're just too many and they've come in too fast for me to keep track."

"How about a lawyer named Abernathy?"

"J. Cornelius?" Foxx nodded, and Morse smiled. "I haven't made up my mind about him yet. He's acting for some of the prospectors, I understand, something to do with the Kansas land laws. He and his clients aren't doing much talking, so that's about all I can say on the subject."

"Is he a good lawyer, or a shyster?"

"Hard to tell. He could be either, for all I know."

"What about a fellow named Ingersoll?"

"Oh, Homer's been here awhile. He's done right well for himself, as far as I know. Buys up an abandoned homestead here and there. Seems to be well-fixed, but I don't know where his money came from, and he's pretty closemouthed about his past." Morse looked at Foxx quizzically. "For a man who just got to town, you seem to've done pretty well in finding things out."

"All I'm doing is the job I'm supposed to. The C&K don't pay me for sitting around wasting time. They expect me to work as fast as I can on a job like this one."

"Oh, I can understand that. You still don't feel like telling me a little more about what you plan to do?"

Foxx shook his head. "If I knew what I was going to have to do to straighten things up here, I'd feel a lot better myself right this minute."

Morse frowned and looked searchingly across the table. Just before Foxx began to feel uncomfortable he said, "You seem to be a sensible man, Foxx."

"Thanks. I try to be."

"I'll pass something on to you, if you'll settle for a flat statement, and not ask me any questions," Morse offered.

Now it was Foxx's turn to look questioningly. The scrutiny didn't disturb Morse. He sat impassive, meeting Foxx's gaze while he drained his glass. Foxx got the idea the reporter was prepared to wait as long as he had to for an answer.

After a moment, Foxx said, "I guess you're calling the shots right now. Go ahead."

"Don't be too quick to accept the way things look on the surface here in Sherman. Do some digging, and don't hesitate to dig deep. You'll have to go deeper than some of those prospectors are, out on the flats, to get to the bottom."

Before Foxx could frame a question, Morse stood up, nodded, and walked out of the saloon.

CHAPTER 6

Foxx watched the batwings swinging after Morse pushed through them, wondering just what the editor had meant by his final, cryptic remark. He gave up after a few minutes and tossed off the last few drops of bourbon that remained in his glass, then picked up his valise and walked over to the bar. Bert had been busying himself polishing the glasses that stood in rows on the bottom shelf of the backbar and re-arranging them. He turned around when Foxx put his empty glass down.

"How'd you get along with Frank?" the barkeep asked.

"Why, I never fight with strangers, Bert. Not unless they lead off with a punch, which Morse didn't. But I'm a mite curious. How's his newspaper regarded hereabouts?"

"Oh, Frank stands pretty good. He don't do a lot of backing and filling, but he can speak his mind real plain when he figures it's called for. When it comes to the paper, I guess it's about the best we can expect, printed way off up in Topeka."

"Morse can be pretty tight-mouthed when he wants to, I noticed."

"Well, nobody's got much use for a blabbermouth, Mr. Foxx."

Foxx nodded. He glanced outside. Darkness had fallen while he and Morse talked, and his stomach had begun reminding him that it'd been a long time since noon, when he'd eaten the sandwiches put up for him by the depot café in Courtland.

"I didn't notice any eating-houses on my way in from the railhead," he said. "But I expect there's a place where a man can get a meal here in town."

"There's two of 'em, but you're too late to go to the best one. That's Miz O'Shea's; she just feeds regulars at her place. If you're going to be here awhile, you'd be well-off taking your meals with her. It's expensive, she gets two-bits apiece for dinner and supper and throws in breakfast, but she sets a better table than Pancake Jack does. Unless you like flapjacks every meal."

"I'll see about getting on as a regular at Mrs. O'Shea's tomorrow. And right now, flapjacks or just about anything else would taste pretty good."

"Oh, Jack's place ain't all that bad. Just gets sorta tiresome if you eat there every meal. It's right across from the livery stable. Miz O'Shea's is that green-painted house just down the street from here."

"I won't have any trouble finding either one." Foxx picked up his valise. "I'll go wash up first, though. Oh, yes. One more thing, Bert. Where'd I be likely to run into a lawyer named Abernathy?"

"Right here in The Union. He rooms here. One

door down from you, in Number Three. Uses the
back corner over there for an office, but he's been
gone since noon today. I imagine he'll show up by
the time you finish supper."

"I'll look for him when I come back, then. But
right now, I need some grub inside me to keep my
belly button from rubbing on my backbone."

When Foxx returned to The Union a half hour
later he was in a more relaxed mood, thanks to a
three-high stack of thick sourdough pancakes with
bacon on the side and several cups of coffee. Even
before he pushed through the swinging doors, the
loud buzz of voices from inside told Foxx that the
saloon was no longer the deserted place it had been
earlier.

There were eight or ten men lined up along the
bar, and Foxx noted that the overalled farmers stood
at one end, the prospectors in their dirt-stiff jeans at
the other, with a wide space separating the two groups.
Several of the tables were occupied, and the same
division between farmer and prospector held true at
them.

Two of the gambling tables were busy, the house
man keeping an eye on a four-handed euchre game
at one table and presiding over a session of draw
poker at the other. In the farthest corner, under the
overhanging balcony, two men sat talking. Foxx shot
a quick glance at them. No great amount of guess-
work was needed for him to decide that while one
of them was probably a prospector, the other had to
be J. Cornelius Abernathy.

At the moment, the lawyer was leaning forward to
bring his head close to that of the man across the

table. Abernathy's face was florid, and looked ruddy-red, framed as it was by a heavy mane of high-combed gray hair and a set of flared-out cavalry sideburns that came down to his jaws. His nose was blunt, his lips full, his jaw round above a pair of extra chins. He wore a gray frock coat over an embroidered vest and the baby-blue cravat that puffed out below the vee of his shirt collar was ornamented with a pearl stickpin. His brow was furrowed and his thick lips moved with slow deliberation as he spoke to his companion.

Bert finished replenishing the glasses of the group of farmers who occupied the front end of the bar and moved down to where Foxx was standing. Without waiting for instructions, he took Foxx's private bottle from the shelf and set it on the bar with a glass beside it.

"I guess you already spotted Abernathy," he said, nodding toward the table in the back.

"I figured that's who it had to be. He wear that getup all the time?"

"Either that one or one just about like it. I suppose the rigout goes with the job, but I'm glad it ain't me who's got to doll up that way when I go to work."

One of the prospectors at the rear end of the bar banged a glass to get Bert's attention. The barkeep hurried down to serve the man. Foxx poured a drink and sipped it while he studied the two men at the rear table. Apparently Abernathy had made whatever point he'd been driving home, for his companion nodded and stood up. Foxx waited until the prospector had left before picking up his bottle and glass and moving back to Abernathy's table.

"You'd be Abernathy, wouldn't you? The lawyer?"

"I am, sir. But I'm afraid you have the advantage."

Abernathy's voice was courtroom-trained, deep and sonorous. It seemed to come from somewhere in the vicinity of his belt-buckle, and though he hadn't spoken loudly, Foxx felt it resonating in his ears. Now, at close range, Foxx could see that the attorney's eyes were the same baby-blue hue as the cravat he wore.

"My name's Foxx. C&K Railroad."

"To be sure. One of my clients told me of your arrival." Abernathy indicated the chair recently vacated by the prospector. "Well, sit down, Mr. Foxx. I'd offer you a tot of brandy, but I see you have your own tipple."

"Thanks just the same."

Foxx sat down and refilled his glass. He took out a stogie and lighted it before drinking. The lawyer sipped from the glass in his hand, waiting for Foxx to begin.

Foxx said, "I guess it was Mercer told you I was here. I visited with him awhile when I run into him out at the diggings on my way into town."

"Ben mentioned it to me, yes," Abernathy nodded. "He was the first, but not the only one. I get the impression that you're here to investigate the possibility of a suit in eminent domain, and force the prospectors to abandon their claims on the railroad's right of way."

"I hate to disappoint you, Abernathy, but I'm not a lawyer. All I was sent here to do is to get construction started again on that spur we're trying to push south."

"Are you warning me, Foxx? Or coming to me for help?"

"Why, neither one. I guess you'd say I'm looking for some way to keep everybody happy and get our rails pushed on at the same time."

Abernathy smiled. "Very clever, Foxx. Your approach fits your name quite well."

"Sounds like you think I'm getting ready to pull some kind of cute trick on your prospector friends, Abernathy. That ain't the way of it. Like I told your man Mercer, it don't matter to us whether we haul wheat or gold ore. Thing is, we can't haul anything until we've got rails laid."

"You'll have to overlook my clients' suspicions, Foxx. They don't have much reason to trust anybody. Except me."

"I'm curious to know if I've got the straight story of how Mercer and his partners happened to make that strike," Foxx said. "When I was talking to him out at the diggings, he spun me a yarn about a water witch leading 'em to it. Sounded pretty thin to me. Is that the truth of how it happened?"

Instead of making a direct reply, Abernathy asked Foxx, "You've heard how Henry Wickenburg found the Vulture lode, out in Arizona Territory?"

"I don't see how it applies, but as I recall the yarn, his burro started to run away and Wickenburg picked up a rock to throw at the critter. Then it struck him the rock was real heavy. He looked at it and seen it shining with free gold. Pure luck was all it was."

"That's my point, Foxx. Don't discount luck. Men like Ben Mercer and Red Simpson have found more gold by accident than all the mining engineers and geologists in the country have ever uncovered setting out to look for it."

"I wouldn't argue that with you," Foxx said. "Go on, Abernathy. You was here the day they hit their strike. I'd like to hear what happened firsthand."

"I wasn't with them, you understand, but I think the story they told the night they discovered the lode was straight enough. As I just said, the strike was an accident. Mercer and Simpson had come here to homestead, and—"

"Just a minute," Foxx broke in. "How'd they happen to pick Sherman outa all the other places where there's better land and more water?"

"Both of them are Kansas boys," Abernathy replied. "Born up in the northeast corner, a little town called Tonganoxie. They got on the wrong side in a dispute with some jayhawkers there, but balked at moving out of Kansas, so they came down here looking for land they could file on. At least, that's what they told me. I won't guarantee it's the truth, and it's not important any longer. Is it?"

"No. I was just wondering. Go ahead."

"I'd never seen them before the night they made the strike," the lawyer went on, "but they certainly drew attention then."

Mercer and Simpson had burst into The Union early in the evening, an hour or so after sunset, Abernathy told Foxx. He'd been sitting at a table just inside the door, and there were only two or three other men in the saloon.

"Clear the tracks!" Mercer had yelled just before they'd hit the batwings. "We're coming through!"

Come through they did, with enough force to send

the swinging doors clapping against the inside walls on both sides. Daisy was riding on Simpson's shoulders. Her long henna-red hair was flying in wild disarray. She had on a low-necked blouse, which had slipped down on one plump shoulder to expose most of one full breast. Her skirt was hiked up around her hips, and her bare legs were streaked with dirt.

"Break out the bottles, Bert!" she called from her perch. "We're all gonna celebrate getting rich!"

"Damn it, Daisy!" Bert said angrily. "Get down from there and make yourself decent! Then get the hell back to your own place where you belong. You know The Union's rules. You girls ain't allowed in here, either to hustle customers or to drink."

"Break your rules tonight, Bert!" Simpson said. In contrast to his partner, who was short and florid, Simpson was tall, broad, lean, and lantern-jawed. "Hell, man, this is the biggest night this town's ever likely to have!"

"Red's telling it straight, Bert," Mercer put in. "Get a move on, now. We want a couple of bottles of the best liquor you got. The drinks are on us tonight!"

One of the men who'd been standing at the bar called, "Go on, Bert. Break your rules if they're standing treat."

Bert hesitated. Abernathy could tell what was going through his mind. It was a slow night, and it was also pretty obvious that Daisy was interested in drinking, not hustling the customers.

"Maybe I'll let you stay, Red," the barkeep finally said. "But show me your money before I start putting out drinks for the house."

Mercer began to guffaw loudly. "We got something better'n money, Bert. Ain't that right, Red?"

"You're damn right it is!" Simpson leaned down and helped Daisy off his shoulders to the bar, where she sat drumming her heels on the front, laughing almost as loudly as Mercer.

For a moment, Abernathy thought the two men were already drunk. They acted like a pair of boisterous schoolboys, laughing over nothing, pounding one another on the back, now and then shaking hands for no apparent reason.

Bert's patience was wearing thin. "Come on, Ben. If you and Red are going to buy for the house, put the money on the bar or shut up."

Mercer dug into the pocket of his overalls and pulled out a handful of pebbles. He tossed them on the bar. They rattled as they scattered over the wooden surface. Bert gazed at them.

"You fellows have got a poor idea of a joke," he told them sourly. "Now pick up your rocks and get out of here. And take Daisy with you."

"Rocks, my ass!" Mercer snorted. "Damn it, Bert, don't you know gold when you see it?"

For a moment, a stunned, unbelieving silence hung over the saloon. Then the half-dozen men in The Union, Abernathy among them, crowded up to look at and finger the misshapen objects that Mercer had tossed out. Both Mercer and Simpson watched them closely as the pebblelike pieces were passed from hand to hand. Bert finally broke the silence.

"Where'd you dig it up, Ben?" he asked.

"That's for us to know and you to find out!"

"Well, if you won't say where, tell us how you come to dig it up," one of the men said.

"No need to beat around the bush on that," Red told the man. "We took Daisy out to see if she could witch us a water-well on a place we aimed to homestead. We dug where her forked stick dipped down, a little ways off from an old buffalo wallow, and there it was. Not water, but gold, and that's better'n water any day, in my book."

Bert asked skeptically, "You say it's gold. How do you know?"

"I'll show you." Mercer carefully collected all the bits that the patrons were fingering curiously. He flicked through them with a finger until he found the one he was looking for, and put the others back in his pocket. Holding the one he'd selected up at eye-level he said, "See here, where I cut into this nugget with my shovel? Look at that color in the cut. If that ain't pure-dee gold, I'll put in with you."

"Sure looks like gold, all right," one of the men said.

"So does a lot of other things," another objected. He dug into a pocket and brought out a handful of coins, from which he took a five-dollar gold piece. He held the coin up to the nugget in Mercer's hand and squinted. Then he snorted with disgust. "Shit! That ain't no more like gold than ditchwater's like whiskey. Look at it!"

Mercer's face puckered into a frown. "You don't know your ass from a hot rock! It still looks like gold to me!"

"I'm with Ben," Simpson said. "It looks like gold to me, too."

"How's a gold miner know for sure when he's digging?" one of the others asked. "There's got to be a way of testing."

"Acid," the man with the gold half eagle replied. "Pour some acid on it. If it's gold, acid won't turn the color or melt it down."

"Where in hell are you going to find acid around here?" Bert asked.

"Old Jake uses some kind of acid in his smithy, down at the livery stable," one of them remembered. He'd know more about it than anybody else in town, anyhow."

"Well, why don't you just run down to the livery, and get Jake to bring some of his acid up here," Bert said. "If Ben and Red have turned up a gold lode here, I guess all of us would be interested in knowing about it. Tell Jake I'll stand the drinks if he'll take the time to come test these rocks."

Electricity filled the air during the time required for a volunteer to hurry down to the livery stable and return with the blacksmith. All the men in the saloon except Abernathy and Bert were proving homestead claims, and the idea that they might be sitting on a new Golconda made them itch with excited eagerness. The messenger returned with Jake, who carried a thick-walled bottle sealed with rubber stopper.

"Can you tell whether these rocks Ben and Red dug up are gold?" Bert asked the smith.

"Sure," Jake replied. "This here's muriatic acid. I use it to etch steel with, when some dude wants a fancy-decorated gun. If you put it on anything but gold, it'll eat hell out of it."

"Now, wait a minute," Mercer protested. "I ain't so sure—"

"Shut up, Ben," Bert snapped. "You started this

with that piece of rock. Now you're going to let Jake test it, whether you like the idea or not."

Reluctantly, Mercer surrendered the nugget to the blacksmith. Jake asked Bert, "You got an empty whiskey bottle I can use? If I pour this stuff on the top of the bar, it'll eat right through the varnish and the wood, too."

Not a sound broke the stillness in The Union as Jake prepared the test. The clink of glass against glass when he poured a quarter-inch of acid into the bottle, and the tiny thunk of the nugget being dropped into the liquid sounded like peals of thunder. Jake tilted the whiskey bottle and sloshed the acid over the nugget; tiny bubbles formed on its surface and a film clouded the acid surrounding it. Slowly, the film dissolved. The nugget gleamed a rich, opulent yellow in the slightly discolored acid.

"My God!" Ben Mercer sighed. "It is gold, Red! Damn it, partner, we're rich!"

"Yep." Jake nodded with satisfaction. "It's gold, right enough. I ain't run into a lot of gold in my life, but I do know it when I see a chunk."

His voice low, Red Simpson asked Ben, "Do you think we ought to get Jake to test the rest of it? Just to make sure?"

Jake stared at the partners. "You mean you got some more of this stuff?"

Wordlessly, Mercer dug out the remaining nuggets. Jake hefted them and then took out a pocketknife. He tested each of the dirt-crusted pieces, first probing with the point of the blade, then scratching into it with the edge. He worked silently, and again the atmosphere in the saloon grew tense, as the men shoved as close to the blacksmith as they could get to miss nothing that he did.

When Jake had finished his testing, he poured the acid from the whiskey bottle back into its container and handed the empty to Bert. "You better bust this up good. Anybody puts drinking water or whiskey in it and drinks outa it, he'll get one hell of a big bellyache."

"Was it all gold, Jake?" Bert asked.

"Every piece of it. After that first one, I didn't need the acid. It's the real thing. Pretty high-test, too. Oughta run up to twenty, maybe twenty-two carat fine."

Bert's jaw dropped. He gasped, "Well, I'll be damned!"

Completely absorbed in Jake's testing, the few who'd been in the saloon from the beginning hadn't been really aware that men had been trickling in, one or two at a time, to join them. In a town as small as Sherman, news moves in fast-spreading ripples, and summoning Jake to test the nuggets had started just such a ripple speeding through the settlement. Now a yell rose that threatened to split the rafters of The Union's roof. A general jostling began, as the latecomers began pushing up to the bar for a closer look at the nuggets.

Mercer and Simpson didn't object to their treasure being inspected, but they took care not to surrender any of the nuggets to the curious. Bert, carried away by Jake's final pronouncement, began setting bottles on the bar at random. After the first few had been emptied within a space of minutes, he came to his senses and began selling drinks again.

The pandemonium that the strike had created kept The Union crowded until daylight.

"And I don't need to tell you what happened after that," Abernathy concluded, gazing across the table at Foxx over the rim of his frequently replenished brandy glass. "The next morning, the town was so thick with men digging that you couldn't stir them with a broomstick. Everywhere—in yards, gardens, even some in the streets."

"Any of 'em find gold?" Foxx asked.

"Oh, yes indeed. Most of it was found within a mile or less of the place where Ben and Red made their strike. You saw that area when you came in from the railhead. They call it 'the diggings' now."

"Have they stopped digging up the streets by now?"

"Oh, it still happens, but not as often as it did for the first week or two. Most of the prospectors go out to the edge of the diggings now."

"I noticed that. But I got the idea there hasn't been much fresh gold found lately. How long you think the fever's going to hold, Abernathy? We need to get that spur moving again."

"Oh, there's still a lot of gold fever in Sherman, Foxx. Don't make any mistake about that. I look for it to last awhile."

"Not that it's any of my affair," Foxx said casually, "but how'd you get into this business?"

"You're too shrewd for me to try to convince you that I'm acting in a spirit of altruism," Abernathy smiled. "My first thought was the legalities involved, so I had a chat with Ben and Red before they got too drunk. And then more prospectors asked me to represent them."

"How's it happen you haven't filed a single claim for any of 'em?" Foxx asked.

"Oh, come now, Foxx! You work for the C&K, I'm sure you know the land laws in the states where the road has interests."

Keeping his face expressionless, Foxx nodded. He hoped that Abernathy wouldn't probe his knowledge of those laws too deeply.

"Before I file any claims, I intend to clear up the vague distinction Kansas law makes between homestead claims and mining claims. After that—well, I'll just have to reserve discussing what we might do."

"You mean you're going to bog everything down in lawyer's red tape, and keep the C&K and the town both tied up!"

"Don't put words in my mouth, Foxx! What I'm saying is that gold is where you find it, and possession is still nine points of the law." Abernathy drained his glass, picked up his bottle of brandy and stood up. "Now I'll bid you good night, Foxx. I don't suppose our talk's eased your mind about the future of your railroad spur, but facts are facts and have to be faced. The facts of this case are that my clients hold all the aces, and your railroad hasn't even got a hand in the game yet. Sleep on it, and perhaps you'll see what I mean."

Foxx watched the lawyer's back as Abernathy went up the stairs and entered his room. Foxx pulled out a fresh stogie and touched a match to it. He puffed at the twisted cigar furiously, until the tendrils of smoke that wreathed his head were as numerous as the unanswered questions running through his mind.

CHAPTER 7

Mrs. O'Shea planted her work-reddened hands on her bony hips and scrutinized Foxx from the crown of his black homburg to the soles of his Nocona-made boots. During his earlier footloose days before he'd gotten firmly rooted in a permanent job, Foxx had undergone similar examinations by other angular, thin-lipped boardinghouse landladies who might have been twin sisters to Mrs. O'Shea. He waited patiently until she nodded her approval.

"You look like a man who'd behave himself in a decent woman's house," she said. "I'll be glad to add you to my regulars, Mr. Foxx."

"Why, thank you, Mrs. O'Shea. It'll be a real relief to be sure I'm going to have good meals while I'm here in Sherman."

"It's twenty-five cents apiece for dinner and supper, and I throw in breakfast. Cold supper on Sundays. Breakfast's from six thirty until eight, dinner at noon and supper at six." Mrs. O'Shea looked pointedly at the clock hanging on the wall of the hallway; the hands stood only ten minutes before eight. "And I don't give special privileges to folks who're late for meals."

"I'll try to be on time after this," he promised.

"It's all the same to me whether you pay by the day or by the week, but I don't serve folks who get behind."

"I don't know how long I'll be here," Foxx said. "Suppose I pay you every three or four days?"

"That's just fine." She took the two silver dollars Foxx handed her and said, "Sit down, then, and I'll dish up some more ham and eggs and get a fresh pan of biscuits."

There was only one other hat on the halltree where Foxx put his homburg before going into the dining room. Foxx recognized the hat's owner when he sat down at the long table; he'd seen Homer Ingersoll the day before in the store. Ingersoll, Foxx saw, was just finishing breakfast; his plate was empty, but he was still chewing, his mouth full. He nodded, and Foxx returned the silent greeting with a nod of his own.

Foxx was not in the best of moods. He'd awakened that morning in his room at The Union with the uncomfortable feeling of frustration that always followed a day that he'd spent groping around in a strange place trying to gather up the loose ends of a new case. Lying in bed, lighting his first stogie, he'd reminded himself that yesterday hadn't been exactly wasted, but even that gave him little satisfaction.

He'd felt only a little better after he'd sponged in the tepid water from the pitcher that stood on the bare little room's washstand, and shaved for the first time in two days. Foxx's stomach had begun growling about that time, and he'd decided that unpacking his valise could wait until later in the day. He'd dressed hurriedly, putting on the clothing he'd worn while traveling.

Both his long-barreled American Model Smith & Wesson and his .44 House Colt were lying where he'd placed them the night before, as he always did in the field, in a chair beside the bed. Instead of belting on the heavy Smith & Wesson, Foxx had donned his coat and slipped the little Cloverleaf Colt into its sewed-in holster in the left inside-breast of the garment. There'd be plenty of time later in the day to put on fresh socks and change boots, he'd told himself.

Now, as he filled a cup with steaming coffee from the big ironware pitcher that stood between him and Ingersoll, the prospects of food made Foxx feel better. Mrs. O'Shea came in carrying a big platter of ham and eggs and a plate of steaming biscuits. Foxx helped himself generously. The smoky fragrance of the ham wafted to his nostrils and his spirits began to improve still more.

Ingersoll swallowed and cleared his throat. He took a sip of coffee before saying to Foxx, "I remember you from yesterday in the store. Kept Eb from killing those prospectors. You move right fast, Mr.—"

"Foxx. And I heard your name yesterday, Mr. Ingersoll."

"Well, now." Ingersoll seemed pleased. "Sort of surprised you'd remember, hearing it just the one time, and as busy as you was right then."

"All the hurry was over by that time."

"So it was. You're here on business, I suppose? Something to do with the new goldfield?"

Foxx had filled his plate and was cutting a bite of the ham. He took his time answering. Ingersoll reached for the pitcher and refilled his cup. He was in no hurry, apparently. Foxx saw that if he was going to enjoy his breakfast in peace, he'd have to satisfy the man's curiosity.

"Only in a roundabout way," he said. "That new goldfield's holding up construction on the spur the C&K's pushing south. I came to see what can be done to get the job moving again."

"You're a C&K man, then." There was satisfaction in Ingersoll's voice. "Glad the railroad's taking an interest. If something isn't done to stop those prospectors, they'll take over our town."

"I don't aim to take sides in this thing, Ingersoll," Foxx said quickly. "The C&K had just as soon haul ore as wheat. But I don't intend to get myself in the middle of a fight between the townsfolk and the prospectors."

Ingersoll shook his head dolefully. "It seems to me that you're going to have more trouble persuading those prospectors to let that line go through their claims than you'd ever have dealing with the people in Sherman. We've known all along where your right of way's going to run."

Foxx had just dipped the bite of ham on his fork into the yolk of one of the eggs on his plate and popped it into his mouth. He studied his table companion as he chewed.

Ingersoll reminded him of a starved crow that had gotten separated from its flock. He wore a black suit and a wide black cravat that almost covered his white shirt. His close-trimmed black beard did nothing to hide the shrunken cheeks of his narrow face, and his nose jutted out like a bird's beak between small beady eyes that had only a narrow rim of white around their pupils.

After swallowing, Foxx replied, "I haven't been here long enough to figure out just exactly how things stack up, but I'll be going out to the diggings today and see what I can find out."

"Well, if I can help you, let me know, Foxx." Ingersoll pushed his chair back and stood up. "I'm as interested as everybody else in town to see Sherman on a railroad."

"Thanks. I'll remember your offer."

After Ingersoll's departure, Foxx finished his breakfast in thoughtful silence, making a mental list of the loose ends he needed to tie up. He'd stepped out to the porch of Mrs. O'Shea's house and was holding a match to his after-breakfast stogie when a gunshot in the distance, followed almost immediately by a second shot, shattered the morning's stillness.

Foxx started walking in the direction from which the shots had sounded. He'd taken only a few steps when the angry crackling of a small fusillade broke out.

By now people were popping out of houses and stores on both sides of the street. Most of the men carried rifles or shotguns; those who didn't were strapping on pistol-belts. The men began moving in the same direction Foxx was walking; the few women who'd appeared stood in the doors of the houses, their eyes following the men.

After the short angry *rat-a-tat* of the fusillade, the shooting had stopped momentarily. Now a single shot rang out, followed by a second, and after a pause, a third.

One of the men hurrying toward the shooting called to another, "Looks like it's finally come to a head!"

"About time, too! Now's our chance to get rid of them damn gold-grubbers once and for all!"

Bert was standing in front of The Union, and as Foxx angled over toward the saloon, Abernathy pushed through the batwings. The attorney was still shrugging into his coat. He was hatless and collarless, and streaks of lather showed white on his chin.

"Foxx!" he said. "If you're heading for where that shooting is, I'll walk with you."

"Come along," Foxx invited. "I don't know what's happening, but I figured I'd better find out."

"Hell, anybody can tell what's going on," Bert put in. "The damn war's started up, that's what. It was bound to happen, the way folks have been feeling."

"It was quiet enough last night," Foxx said.

"Before you went up to bed, it was," Bert told him. "Then a new bunch of prospectors blew in a little bit after midnight. I guess they must've got pushy and touched it off."

Abernathy cocked his head to listen and said hopefully, "Things seem to've quieted down now, though."

Almost before he'd finished speaking, another shot split the air. Foxx said, "It's not over yet. If you still want to go see what's happening, Abernathy, let's move."

They joined the straggle of men, fewer now in numbers, who were hurrying toward the edge of town. When they reached the embankment that sep-

arated Sherman's houses from the diggings, they saw
that the goldfield was almost totally deserted. Only
a handful of prospectors were to be seen, and they
were not working. To a man, they were running parallel with the embankment at right angles to Sherman's main street.

"Whatever's going on is off to our left," Foxx told
his companion. He pointed to the west. Behind the
earthen barricade the heads of the prospectors and
the barrels of the rifles and shotguns they held made
a ragged line.

"Good God! They're facing off for a pitched battle!" Abernathy gasped. "Foxx, I've got to stop this!
A lot of those men are my clients! I can't let them
start a war with the homesteaders!"

A shot sounded, its source invisible to them, and
a spurt of dirt rose from the earthworks shielding the
prospectors. The men ducked out of sight, then one
the fire. They were aiming at the houses that stood
off the main street, parallel to the embankment.

"Looks to me like they've already started one,"
Foxx said. "And if we ain't careful, we're going to
be caught between 'em!"

Underscoring Foxx's warning, a shotgun boomed
from the barricade directly ahead of them. A dust-
cloud blossomed in the dusty street where its pellets
hit, a few yards from where they stood.

"Get behind them houses!" Foxx urged. "If that'd
been a rifle with the range to reach us, we'd've been
hit!"

With Abernathy close behind him, Foxx scurried
for cover behind the nearest house. Off the main
street, the houses that straggled to the western edge

of Sherman stood in a wavering line between the ruts of a track that, if straight, could have been called a street. Most of the houses were soddies, their thick earth walls as impervious to bullets as a fort. The townsmen had divided into small groups of three or four or a half-dozen, each bunch using one of the dwellings for cover, peering around its sides at the prospectors behind their earthworks.

In back of one of the soddies, the men using its shelter were bending over the recumbent form of one of their number. Abernathy shook his head and said unhappily, "That's what I've been afraid of. Blood's been spilled, Foxx. Once that happens, things begin to get out of hand."

"We'll work our way from house to house and see how bad it is," Foxx said.

Shots were still being fired occasionally as Foxx and the lawyer dodged across the open spaces between the houses to where the casualty lay. As far as they could tell, looking ahead, no one else had been hit. Abernathy began pushing through the ring of men around the one who'd been wounded. Foxx followed him. He recognized the man lying on the ground; it was Slim Edwards, the tall, thin deputy marshal he'd talked with the previous day. The deputy was propped up to raise his shoulders off the ground, a bloodstained towel wrapped around his thigh. He recognized Foxx and nodded.

"Can I do anything for you, Slim?" Foxx asked.

"I don't know what it'd be." Edwards moved and a grimace of pain swept across his face. "The way my leg feels, I won't be doing much dancing for a while, but I'll make out, Foxx."

"Does the marshal know you got hit?"

"Somebody's looking for him now. Ed stood night-watch last night. I don't guess he's had more'n about an hour's sleep. And there's somebody gone after Granny Blossom, too."

"Granny Blossom?"

"She's the closest thing we got here to a doctor. But I'd as soon she took care of me as any regular sawbones."

"All right, you men! Clear away, let me through!"

Foxx looked around. The speaker was a burly man wearing a wide-brimmed hat. A star was pinned on his vest, and he carried a revolver in his hand. The men around the wounded deputy gave ground. He bent over Edwards.

"You all right, Slim?" he asked.

"I reckon. Leg's throbbing like hell, is all."

"You see who it was shot you?"

"Not a chance. I'd just stepped out from behind the house, I was going out to try to stop the shooting, and about three of 'em cut down on me at the same time."

"How'd all this start?" the marshal asked Edwards.

"You know about that bunch of prospectors that got in late last night, because it was you who told me about 'em."

"Close to twenty of 'em," the marshal nodded. "I warned 'em to stay outa trouble."

"Did you know somebody'd dug up a nugget or two yesterday, on the town side of that dirt bank they've put up?"

Parsons shook his head. "No. Damn it, Slim, you mean you let them fellows dig on the town side of that bank?"

"They started while I was down at the other end.

I chased 'em back into the diggings, soon as I saw 'em. Anyhow, the new bunch, and some of the old ones, too, I guess, started digging around the houses. They wouldn't back off when the men that lived in the houses told 'em to."

"I was the first one that told 'em to git," one of the onlookers volunteered. "And when they didn't git, I went in and come back out with my gun. Let off a shot over their heads. They got, then."

"Yeah," said another man. "I seen the whole thing. And when I heard Fleet's shot, I come out with my gun to back him up. And it just got worse from then on."

"Damn gold-grubbers started coming at us from every whichaway," the man named Fleet continued. "Then my neighbors seen what was going on, and come to help."

"That's about the time I got here," the deputy said. "I guess that's about all there was to it, Ed."

From somewhere down the line of houses a shot sounded, and a moment later another shot replied.

"Look here, Ed," Abernathy said, "you've got to stop this before somebody's killed."

"Just keep your dick in your jeans, Abernathy," the marshal replied. "I'll do what's necessary, don't worry."

From behind Foxx, one of the men spoke. "What we oughta do is all march out there together and send them goddamn prospectors kiting their asses outa here!"

"Damn right!" another agreed.

"Now, you fellows cool down!" Parsons commanded. "Fleet, I want you to go in and get a white cup-towel or a pillowcase from your missus. Then I'll see what I can do to stop this fracas."

"You mean you're going to dicker with the bastards?"

Foxx thought the voice sounded off-key; he looked around to locate the speaker. There'd been only five or six men in the group around the wounded deputy when he and Abernathy arrived, but now it had grown to a dozen or more as men from the adjoining houses had come to find out what was going on. Foxx quickly spotted the man who'd spoken; those nearest him were looking at him admiringly and nodding in agreement.

There was nothing of the homesteader in the newcomer's looks. Instead of the overalls that were the common denominator of Sherman's male residents, he wore a frock coat and string necktie and a pair of fawn-hued buckskin cloth trousers. Habit led Foxx's eyes to his boots. They were not the scarred, unpolished clodhopper boots of a farmer. At a guess, Foxx placed the maker who'd produced them as being a northern cattle country boot-man, from Wyoming or Montana.

Ed Parsons had been studying the newcomer with a scrutiny as close as Foxx's. Now the marshal said, "I'll thank you to butt outa this, mister. Let the home-folks and me settle things."

"Sorry, Marshal," the stranger said. He touched a finger to the wide brim of his flat-crowned hat. "It wasn't my idea to interrupt the cause of peace and justice. If that's what you hope to get by talking."

"He's right, Ed," one of the men growled. "Them fellows out there in the diggings don't talk our language."

"They'll talk to me," Parsons snapped. He turned to Fleet. "Now get me that white cloth I asked for, and I'll go parley."

His face dour, Fleet disappeared into the house. Parsons looked at the men clustered around him. He saw the lawyer. "You're on good terms with the prospectors, Abernathy. You come along with me. Maybe they'll listen to you."

"I don't—" Abernathy began, then pressed his lips together and said, "All right, Ed. You must be right. I'll do what I can to help."

"Now, I want two or three of you other men to go out there with me to talk for the folks in town. You're going to tell them prospectors that as long as they stay on their side of the deadline, you'll leave 'em alone." He pointed at one of the homesteaders. "You, Bob. And Walt, you come with us, too."

"Not me." The first man the marshal had chosen shook his head. "I don't want any part of promising them sons of bitches we'll ease up on 'em."

"I'm standing with Bob, Marshal," Walt said firmly. "If any of us goes out there, we'll go out shooting, and chase their asses all the way down to No Man's Land where they belong."

A mutter of general agreement rose from the others. Parsons scanned the faces of the men staring at him. Foxx, his eyes following those of the marshal, saw in each face the same determination not to appease the prospectors.

"Damn it!" Parson grated, "what's wrong with you men? The way you act, you want a fight! You better think about them men out in the diggings storming into town and tearing things up, if you don't settle things right here and now!"

For a moment, nobody replied, then the newcomer who'd clashed with Parsons earlier broke the strained silence. "Hell, Marshal, everybody wants to see this business settled, but these men want to settle it their way. Not yours."

"That's right!" Bob agreed. "You stand with us, we'll stand with you. But that's how it'll have to be!"

Murmurs of agreement came from the others. Then a silence fell on the group. Abernathy broke it, saying, "Look here, Ed, you're wasting time. Those men out there won't listen to anybody from Sherman, anyhow. What you need is somebody who's not on either side, somebody neutral."

"And who in hell might that be?" Parsons demanded.

"This man right here." The lawyer pointed to Foxx. "Mr. Foxx is from the C&K Railroad."

Parsons turned to look at Foxx. "You're the fellow Slim told me about, then. Except he said you was a railroad detective. Is that right?"

"Yes. But I don't spend all my time chasing crooks. I was sent down here as—well, I guess you'd say as a troubleshooter."

"You'd sure as hell be shooting down a lot of trouble if you can help settle this mess we've got on our hands," Parsons said.

"Wait a minute!" Foxx protested. "I don't want the C&K to get caught in the middle of this fuss, even if what you just said is true. All we want is to see things settled so we can go back to laying rails."

"And the C&K can't move an inch until this fight's settled," Abernathy said quickly. "Isn't that true, Foxx?"

"Yes. It's true enough," Foxx admitted.

Abernathy pressed his advantage. "Go ahead, Foxx. Tell Ed what you said to me last night, about the railroad being as interested in seeing gold mining develop here as it is in the farmers growing good wheat crops."

Parsons nodded slowly. "I can see that'd be the case. And the railroad's got a lot of land-grant sections around here that the state give 'em, ain't that right, Foxx?"

Foxx made time to think by lighting a stogie. He felt that he was being backed into a corner, but decided the best way out of it was to tell the truth. He nodded agreement and said, "There's not anything secret about the land subsidies the C&K's getting, Parsons. Hell, there wouldn't be no railroads out here if it wasn't for them sections of land we get for every mile of track we put down."

Parsons eyed Foxx thoughtfully. "It seems to me like you'd be right interested in getting things settled here, then. Only thing that bothers me is, how far can you go in talking for the railroad?"

"Well, I can't talk like the president or general superintendent could," Foxx replied. "But if they didn't expect me to talk for the road, I wouldn't be here."

"I guess that's as much answer as I need," Parsons nodded. "How about it, Foxx? Will you walk out there with me and the lawyer and talk to them men?"

Knowing that Abernathy had stacked the deck against him, Foxx agreed reluctantly. "I don't know that what I'd say can help you much, but I guess it's part of my job."

Parsons nodded. "Good. We'll go out as soon as Fleet gets here with that cloth I sent him for."

"I'm right here, Marshal," Fleet said. "Just been waiting till you made up your mind who'd be going with you." He handed Parsons a strip of stained white cloth. "Here. It's the best Martha had handy."

"One of you men lend me a rifle or shotgun," Parsons said. When a rifle was offered, he took the gun and tied the cloth to its muzzle. He looked at Foxx and Abernathy. "Well. If you men are ready, I guess we might as well go see what we can do."

CHAPTER 8

Parsons pushed the muzzle of the rifle around the corner of the house and waved it; the strip of white fluttered gently in the still air. For a moment it seemed that no one from the diggings was going to acknowledge the signal, then a voice called, "All right. Come on out. There won't be no shooting from over here, if all you wanta do is jawbone."

"That's what we got in mind," Parsons called back.

He stepped into the space between the two dwellings, and with Foxx and Abernathy flanking him, started walking slowly toward the diggings. All along the embankment, the prospectors were standing, watching. None of them had put down their weapons, though, and on every face he looked at Foxx saw anger and suspicion. A few yards from the earthen barricade, the marshal stopped.

"You men got somebody to talk for you?" he asked the prospectors.

"Ben Mercer's on his way," one of the miners replied. "All of us trusts him not to get us out on any kind of limb."

"Ben's a good choice," Abernathy said. "And I see a lot of you who've come to me for help in getting your claims filed, too. You know I won't sell you out."

Although Foxx had spent only a few minutes the previous day talking with the prospectors' unofficial leader, he recognized Mercer at once when he saw him walking along the edge of the diggings toward the knot of gold seekers that had formed in back of the barricade where the parley was being held.

Following Mercer came a stream of men from the western end of the diggings. Others were joining the group from the other end of the earthen barrier. The embankment was deserted now on both sides of the point where Parsons and Abernathy and Foxx stood, and the prospectors were packed eight or ten men deep behind the long hump of earth that marked the deadline between the claims and the town.

Mercer pushed his way through the prospectors to the front of the crowd. His eyes moved from Parsons to Abernathy to Foxx, and he acknowledged each of them with an individual nod.

"Well, Marshal," Mercer said, "it don't take much brains to know what we've got to talk about. I guess most of us on this side knows this shooting's bad business. But you're the one that wanted to talk, so go ahead and start. We're listening."

"What's it going to take to stop the fighting, Ben?" Parsons asked soberly. "You and the folks from town have both lucked out, so far. Nobody's been killed yet. But if everybody don't lay down their guns, somebody's sure as hell going to be."

"It wasn't us that started the shooting," Mercer replied. "It was one of the fellows from the town side."

"That's right," Parsons agreed. "But he didn't shoot until your men jumped on the wrong side of the boundary and started to dig around his house."

"That was some new fellows, Marshal. They didn't know the rules we agreed to."

"Sure, but how many new men like 'em come into the diggings every day? Ten? Twenty? Don't you tell 'em what's what?"

"We try. These got in late at night. Nobody had a chance to tell 'em anything."

"You think you can keep things in hand better from now on?"

"We can sure try," Mercer said. "Listen, Marshal, you can ask Mr. Abernathy there; we're not looking for trouble. All we want is to be let alone so we can work our claims."

"I know you and your friends don't want any fighting, Ben," Abernathy said. "But the marshal's right about one thing. If any of you start trying to push the diggings into town, there's going to be more trouble. I've warned you about that, remember."

One of the men behind the embankment called, "Whose side are you on now, Abernathy? It sure don't sound to me like you're on ours!"

"Yeah!" another yelled from far back in the group. "What'd you do, sell us out to the sodbusters?"

"Nobody's sold you out!" Abernathy retorted.

"Like hell!" came another shout from behind the embankment. "All of us seen you come out here from the sodbusters' side!"

While the shouting-match between the lawyer and

prospectors had been developing, the men farthest
back in the group clustered behind the earthworks
had gradually started milling and pushing, as those
in the back tried to get closer to the front of the
barrier.

There was more than one reason for their movement, Foxx found when a sound behind him drew
his attention and he glanced over his shoulder. The
homesteaders had responded to the angry exchange
by coming from behind the houses to hear and see
better. By the time Foxx looked around, the townsmen had crowded into vacant spaces between the
dwellings. Now they were inching still farther forward, spilling out into the strip of clear ground that
separated the town from the diggings.

He turned to warn Parsons. "Marshal, you'd better—" he began, but his warning was never finished.

A shot cracked from behind the barricade. Parsons'
body jerked with the impact of the slug. Slowly, the
marshal crumpled to the ground.

Foxx's fine-honed instincts sent him exploding into
action a few seconds faster than the prospectors and
the homesteaders. While most of them were still
looking around in stunned surprise, trying to locate
the source of the shot, Foxx grabbed the fallen marshal's arm and began dragging him toward the houses.

"Give me a hand, fast!" he snapped to Abernathy,
who was still standing frozen in the center of the
strip of cleared ground. "Move, man! Before all hell
busts loose!"

Foxx's urgent words jarred the lawyer into movement. He took Parsons' other arm and joined Foxx
in dragging Parsons to cover.

With both men pulling the marshal's limp body

they moved faster. Running at a crouch, they reached
the line of houses and got safely behind the nearest
before the belated, scattered shots fired by the few
who recovered quickly from their surprise became a
general exchange of gunfire that sent hot lead whiz-
zing across the strip between the diggings and the
town.

Although Foxx hadn't taken time to plan a course
for their retreat, they'd wound up behind the same
sod house from which they'd gone out for the parley.

Slim Edwards still lay on the ground; a sunbon-
neted woman bending over him. There were twice
as many men behind the soddie now as there had
been when the group left, Foxx noticed. Looking
along the line of houses, he saw that there had been
a similar increase in the number of homesteaders behind them; as the firing continued, Foxx realized,
more and more men from the town had come to join
the fighting.

There were now a dozen men behind the soddie
where Foxx and Abernathy had dragged Parsons.
They were divided into two groups of approximately
equal size, at each end of the dwelling. They paid
little attention to Foxx and Abernathy; their attention was focused on the earthen barrier that sheltered
the prospectors.

"You'd be Granny Blossom?" Foxx called to the
woman attending Edwards. She nodded without looking up from the bandage she was wrapping around
the deputy's wounded leg. Foxx went on, "We got
Ed Parsons here, and he needs looking at. He's pretty
bad hit."

"I'll be there in a minute," she replied. "Where's
he shot?"

"In his chest."

"Well, get his shirt off, if you want to save me some time."

Abernathy kneeled beside Parsons, across from Foxx. Between them, they held up the unconscious man while getting off his vest and shirt. Foxx looked at the wound, a small red pucker high on the right side of Parsons' chest. A thin ribbon of blood trickled from the almost invisible bullet hole. Behind them the rattle of shots continued. The reports were spaced further apart now, as both the prospectors and the homesteaders sought targets rather than firing at random.

Abernathy looked at Foxx and asked, "What do you think?"

Foxx shook his head. "I don't lay claim to knowing much about doctoring. It's plumb outside my line."

Granny Blossom came up to them just in time to hear Foxx's remark. She dropped a small satchel to the ground beside the wounded man and said tartly, "Then git out of my way, so's I can see what's what."

Foxx and Abernathy moved aside. Though the day wasn't warm, the lawyer pulled out a handkerchief and mopped perspiration off his face. Foxx took a stogie from his pocket and lighted it.

Granny Blossom knelt at the side of the marshal and inspected the wound, her eyes only inches from it. She muttered something under her breath, her voice too low for Foxx and the lawyer to catch. Then she began prodding Parsons' chest with her fingertips, moving her wrinkled hands gently across the bare skin of his sternum, stopping now and then to press down gently, retracing their path at such times, tracing the outlines of muscles and ribs.

She looked up at Foxx and asked, "How far away was he from the man that shot him?"

"I can't say. I was looking back toward town when it happened, and whoever shot him was in the diggings."

"I didn't see where the shot came from, either," Abernathy volunteered.

Slim Edwards had been watching them. He called, "How bad is Ed hurt?"

"Can't tell you that yet, young man," Granny answered. "And there ain't a thing you can do about it. I want you to keep still and lay quiet, right where you are."

Dropping her voice to a whisper, Granny said to Foxx and Abernathy, "I wasn't saying that jest to keep Slim from worrying."

"You really don't know?" Foxx asked.

"Not right yet. It depends on whichaway the bullet went into him, and that's what I'm still trying to find out."

Granny abandoned the examination to reach into her satchel and produce a pair of forceps. The long pincerlike instrument was no stranger to Foxx. Bullet wounds were among the hazards of his job, and he'd had his flesh probed with forceps more often than he liked to remember.

Ignoring the scattered firing that still continued, Foxx and Abernathy concentrated on Granny Blossom's moves as she wiped the forceps on her skirt and bent over the recumbent form of the still-unconscious Parsons.

There was no way of telling how old she was, Foxx thought. Under the protruding rim of her bonnet, her face was a network of deep seams, wrinkles on top of wrinkles in a crisscrossing maze. Her eyebrows had thinned with age to an almost invisible line no more than two hairs wide; her eyes were small and brown and snapping-bright, her nose a tiny button between two fleshless lumps of cheekbone. Her thin lips were tightly compressed.

Placing the closed jaws of the forceps on the bullet hole, she inserted the instrument slowly into Parsons' chest. Though still unconscious, the wounded man began to twitch when the metal shaft entered the wound. As the forceps went deeper, Granny's knuckles grew white from the pressure she was exerting. She stopped once to massage her right hand, and then went back to the delicate task of inserting the forceps along the path torn by the bullet in Parsons' flesh.

Parsons started to shudder convulsively. Granny let go of the handle of the forceps. From the hole where the probe entered the marshal's chest, a gush of dark blood welled, puddled momentarily in the crater the instrument had made around it, and trickled in a scarlet line down Parsons' side. The blood flowed for a moment and stopped, and now pink bubbles began forming around the forceps shank. Foxx watched them swell and burst and new bubbles push up. Sighing, Granny pulled the instrument out with a single sweep and clamped her free hand over the bullet hole.

"What's the matter?" Abernathy asked.

"I don't dast probe no deeper for the bullet, that's what's the matter," she snapped. "It's tore clear through his lungs and maybe made a hole in his heart."

Foxx frowned. "Wouldn't he be dead by now if his heart had been hit?"

Granny shook her head. "I seen men live with a bullet clean through their hearts, when I was nursing for the Sanitary Commission during the war. A body just can't tell what a bullet's done to a man. Not without opening him up. Which I can't do, even if I did see some doctors try it."

Parsons moaned. His eyelids fluttered and he moved his hands as though he were feeling for something to hold on to. His eyes opened and he tried to sit up.

Granny Blossom restrained him with a hand on his shoulder. She slid her other hand into one of his, and said, "Now jest lay quiet, Ed. It's all right."

"I—I guess I got shot, didn't I?" he asked her.

"I guess you just did," she replied flatly. "Lay quiet, now. I'll bandage you up in a minute."

"Damn it, Granny, I can't lay quiet!" Parsons protested. "Listen to that shooting! And I'm the only one that can stop it, with Slim shot, too!"

Hearing the marshal's voice, Edwards called, "Don't worry about the shooting, Ed! Let the damn fools kill each other off! And don't worry about me, neither. From the looks of things, you're hurt a lot worse'n I am."

"I can't let them men keep fighting, Slim!" Parsons replied. His hand twitched as he raised it to his chest and found only bare skin. "Where's my badge?"

"It's pinned on your vest, right where it was," Foxx told him. "We had to take your vest and shirt off so Granny could tend to you."

Granny Blossom flipped over the marshal's vest

and unpinned the badge. She held it where Parsons could see it. He held his hand up, and she pressed the metal star into his palm. He lifted the badge up where he could look at it, but the exertion started him coughing. He let the hand holding the badge drop to the ground, and lay still until the coughing spell subsided. Then he held the badge out to Foxx.

"Take my badge, Foxx!" Parsons gasped. He coughed again, and a gush of bright blood burst from his lips. Granny Blossom wiped it away with the palm of her hand. Between choking, wheezy gasps, Parsons went on, "I'm naming you marshal in my place, Foxx. You ain't exactly a lawman, but you're the nearest thing to one in Sherman."

"Now, hold on!" Foxx began.

Parsons cut him short. "No. Somebody's got to take charge. Got to do it right now, too! Take the badge, Foxx! Do what you got to do—"

Again blood poured from the marshal's mouth, choking off his words. He kept trying to speak, but no words came out. Then his body twisted in a quivering convulsion and he lay still, his eyes staring sightlessly at Foxx.

"Ed's dead," Granny Blossom said, her voice flat.

Foxx looked at Abernathy. The lawyer said soberly, "He didn't have any right to put the load he did on you, Foxx."

"No. I'll agree he didn't have the right, but I guess he figured he had some kind of duty."

Slim Edwards spoke up. "Ed had all the right in the world to hand you his badge, Foxx. Like he said, with me laid up, you're the closest thing to a lawman hereabouts."

"Now, wait a minute, Slim," Foxx told the deputy, "there's got to be a sheriff in this county. Or a mayor or somebody in town, here. They're the ones to name somebody to take over from Parsons."

"Sherman never has had a mayor," the deputy said. "Folks just get together and talk about what they need to do to keep the town running, which ain't an awful lot. And the county seat's a day's ride to the east. Sheriff's lazy as a full-bellied pup, anyhow. You wouldn't get much help outa him."

"What're you going to do?" Abernathy asked Foxx.

Foxx jerked his head toward the two groups of men at the ends of the soddie, who were still letting off an occasional shot aimed at the prospectors. He looked both ways along the straggling line of houses; behind most of them, the other groups of homesteaders were doing the same thing. One of the men behind the next house fired while Foxx and Abernathy watched, and an answering slug thudded into the soddie's thick walls and buried itself.

"Somebody's got to take hold, or there's going to be more than Parsons killed."

"It's not your responsibility," Abernathy pointed out.

"Maybe not. And I sure didn't ask for it. I reckon I'm sort of old-fashioned, though. I feel like a dying man's got a right to have his last wish carried out."

"You're going to put on the badge, then?"

"I ain't got much choice, have I?"

"Not the way you look at it. Well, if you're willing to try, the least I can do is help."

"Thanks for not waiting for me to ask you."

"You can count on me, too, Foxx," Edwards volunteered. "Even if I ain't good for very much right now."

"Thanks, Slim. But all I want you to do is just stay still. You don't want that bullet hole in your leg to open up."

"Where do you plan to start?" Abernathy asked.

Foxx looked around. Granny Blossom had put the forceps in her satchel, and was draping Parsons' shirt over his face. The men at the house-corners, absorbed in their fighting, had been paying no attention to what had been happening behind them. Their attention was still riveted on the prospectors.

"Everybody says the best place to start's at home. I take that to mean right here."

Foxx started for the nearest corner of the soddie. After a momentary hesitation, the lawyer followed him. As he walked, Foxx pinned the marshal's badge on his coat lapel. He stopped at the soddie's back wall and put a hand on the shoulder of the man closest to him. The homesteader jumped with surprise and then, after looking at Foxx for a moment, turned around.

Before the man could begin asking questions, Foxx said, "I want you men to quit shooting. Right this minute. And I want one of you to go down the backs of them houses on the right and tell everybody else to hold up firing."

"Like hell I'll stop shooting!" the man snorted. "Not as long as them sonsabitches in the diggings are shooting at us!"

Hearing the angry voice of their companion, the other men turned around. One of them was Fleet. He said, "Who're you to be telling us what to do?" Then he saw the badge on Foxx's coat. "And how come you wearing that badge? What happened to Ed Parsons?"

"Parsons is dead."

"You mean that shot he taken killed him?" Fleet asked.

"Yes."

"And after that you're still telling us to quit shooting at 'em?" Fleet demanded.

"You heard what I said," Foxx replied levelly. "And I want one of you to go to the right along the houses, like I just asked you to, and pass the word for everybody else to quit, too."

"Use your heads, men!" Abernathy urged. "If you don't stop, how in the hell is Foxx going to get the prospectors to stop?"

"Well, now, we don't give a shit whether they stop or not, Mr. Lawyer Man!" snorted one of Fleet's companions. "The longer they keep shooting, the more chance we've got to get rid of 'em!"

"And the more chance they've got to get rid of you!" Abernathy snapped. "Did you ever think of that?"

"We'll take our chances," Fleet told Abernathy.

"Who's going to look after your family if your luck turns bad?" Abernathy asked. "Hadn't you better think about them?"

Fleet found no quick retort for the lawyer's question. Foxx said, "I don't see that you men got anything to lose by holding your fire while I go talk to them prospectors. If they don't promise to put their guns down, you've got my word you can start fighting again, until every damned one of you gets killed.

"Ah, don't pay no attention to this lily-liver, Fleet!" the man standing beside him said. "He can't make us do nothing we don't feel like." He indicated

Foxx's hip, flat under the close-fitting skirt of his coat. "Shit! He ain't even got a gun!"

"No, but I sure have. Morgan!" Edwards called from where he lay. "And I can trigger it faster'n you can swing up your rifles! Now, you do like Foxx tells you!"

All of the homesteaders turned to look, as did Foxx and Abernathy. Slim Edwards was propped on his left elbow. His right hand held a revolver that was trained on the group, its muzzle rock-steady.

Edwards went on, "You men know I'm a middling good shot. If you want me to prove it, just make a move."

None of them acted at all inclined to accept the deputy's challenge.

"You ain't bein' fair, Slim," Morgan complained. "Throwin' down on us while we wasn't looking!"

"Yeah," Fleet chimed in. "All we was trying to do was get back at the bastards that killed poor old Parsons!"

"There was only one shot fired," Foxx said. "All them men in the diggings sure as hell didn't kill him." He eyed the hostile homesteaders coldly. "Now, I want to know if you're going to do what I asked you to, or if I've got to do it myself?"

There was silence for a moment, punctuated only by a shot or two from somewhere along the embankment. The angry homesteaders consulted with their eyes. Finally they reached an unspoken agreement.

"We'll do it, Marshal or Foxx or whatever in hell you expect us to call you," Morgan said grudgingly. "But we sure as hell won't like it!"

"Don't you think I ought to go along with them, when they go along the houses and tell the others to stop firing?" Abernathy asked. "Just to make sure they pass on the message they're supposed to?"

Foxx shook his head. "No. If they've said they'll pass on the word, I'll trust 'em to do it. They look like honest men to me." He turned from Abernathy to face the men. Most of them were staring at him in gap-jawed surprise at his willingness to trust them. Foxx went on, "I don't think I've got you men pegged wrong. But if you don't tell everybody exactly what I've told you to, you can be damn sure I'll look you up when I get back. Now go ahead and let's see if we can't get this shooting stopped!"

Morgan and the other man, whose names Foxx had never heard, started out. Foxx said to Fleet, "I imagine there'll be some of them fellows up the line who've got a scratch or two. I'd be grateful if you'd sorta give Granny Blossom a hand when she gets to patching 'em up."

"Sure, Marshal. I'll be glad to," Fleet replied quickly.

Foxx turned to Abernathy. "Well, I guess it's time for us to go out there and try our luck."

"I'm as ready as I'll ever be," the lawyer replied.

Side by side, they walked through the space between the houses and started across the cleared strip toward the diggings. As they left the shelter of the dwellings, a shot sounded from somewhere to their right. Ahead of them the muzzles of the prospectors' rifles stuck up at ragged intervals above the earth barricade. Foxx strode steadily along, but he didn't remember a time in the past when he'd felt as naked as he did just at that minute.

CHAPTER 9

Instead of coming to a halt in the center of the cleared ground between the houses and the embankment, Foxx kept walking until he and Abernathy were within ten feet of the barricade. When it became obvious that they had no intention of stopping, a half-dozen of the prospectors, those immediately in front of the pair, popped up and leveled their guns at them. Foxx felt better when he saw that Mercer was among them.

"That's far enough!" Mercer commanded. "Stop right where you are."

Foxx and Abernathy halted. Foxx said, "You don't need the guns, Mercer. We've come to talk, not fight."

Mercer nodded. "We figured when we seen you coming that you was after another palaver. Don't see why you'd bother, though. The last one sure didn't do no good."

"Maybe we can do better this time, Ben," Abernathy said.

As had been the case when they'd had the earlier parley, the prospectors had begun standing up when the firing from the houses died away. Then, on seeing Foxx and Abernathy approaching the embankment, they'd started gathering at the middle of the barricade to listen. Before the three men had time to do more than exchange greetings, the space around and behind Mercer was filled with prospectors crowding shoulder to shoulder.

Mercer looked at Foxx with open curiosity. "How'd you get into this thing?" he asked. "You work for the railroad. You don't even live in that damn sodbuster town."

Foxx replied for the benefit of all those listening, "That oughta say something to you men," Foxx replied. "I'm not on anybody's side. All I'm trying to do is get me and the C&K out from the middle of this fuss."

"How come you got on that badge, then?" asked one of the prospectors standing beside Mercer. "What happened to the regular town marshal?"

Foxx had taken a stogie from his pocket. He lighted it before replying. Then, keeping his voice neutral and his eyes fixed on Mercer, he announced, "Parsons is dead."

Mercer frowned. "The hell you say!"

"Most of you seen him hit," Foxx went on. "The shooter was over in the diggings."

"Are you saying one of us killed him?" Mercer asked.

"I'm not saying anything except that the shot came from over here. I didn't see anybody pull the trigger, so I don't know who it was."

An angry murmur rose from the prospectors. Mercer hushed them with a gesture. He said to Foxx, "You remember the way things stood when the slug hit Parsons. All of us was out here, about where we are now, not along the bank or back in the diggings. Anybody could've sneaked over the bank on either side of us and shot him."

Abernathy made an effort at conciliation. "We know that, Ben. Foxx isn't accusing anybody."

"He didn't miss it far," one of the men said angrily.

"If you was listening to what I said," Foxx told the prospectors, keeping his voice low and level, "you'll remember I didn't accuse nobody. What I did say is that the marshal wasn't killed in a fair and square face-down. He was murdered. And murder breeds murder."

"Hell, we all know that, Foxx," Mercer replied impatiently. "There's not a man of us that don't remember how the war started, night riders and bushwhackers and jayhawkers and all of it."

"Then you know that if the shooting don't stop, there'll be more killing," Foxx pointed out. "And if things get too bad out of control, somebody's going to send word to Fort Hays, and there'll be troops movin' in."

"Oh, we'll help you dig out the bastard that killed Parsons, don't worry about that. He put us all in a pickle." Mercer hesitated, and then added, "Don't count too heavy on settling this thing easy, Foxx. Not this time. We're plumb outa patience with the sodbusters. The boys here are just about ready to go into town and wipe things up."

"That'd be a foolish thing to try, Ben," Abernathy
said. "If you men decided to do something like that,
there'd be a real war, and troops taking over here,
just as Foxx said. You don't want that, do you?"

"It'd sure as hell get things settled," one of the
men standing near Mercer said belligerently. "Damn
it, we want to work our claims, not fight all the
time."

Foxx ignored the prospector who'd spoken and
said to Mercer, "There's a good way and a bad way
to cure anything. Maybe we went about it wrong,
before. The men back there in Sherman are ready
to try again if you are." Foxx noticed that the shooting from the houses had now stopped entirely. He
motioned toward the houses behind them. "I guess
you noticed, they ain't shooting back there any more."

"That don't mean a thing," Mercer replied sourly.
"We had the shooting stopped before, too. Started
again real fast, though, if you remember."

"It didn't start until after that shot from over
here killed the marshal," Foxx pointed out.

"That shouldn't ought've happened the way it
did." Mercer shook his head. "I'd give a handful of
nuggets to get my hands on whoever it was done
that."

"I'm going to be looking for him, too," Foxx promised. "Just as soon as we can break up the fighting.
And that's what we're trying to do now, except we
ain't getting very far."

"We're still listening," Mercer said. "Go on, Foxx.
Tell us what you got in mind."

While they'd talked, Foxx had been trying to think
of a plan that might work. He said slowly, impro-
vising as he went along, "how'd it be if you men put

all your guns in a pile out in the middle of that bare space, and—"

"Not a chance!" Mercer broke in.

A murmur of agreement rose from the prospectors who stood close enough to have heard Foxx's suggestion.

Foxx went on quickly, "Wait'll I finish, damn it! If the men from Sherman put all their guns in a pile right by yours, and I get a couple of C&K men from the track gang to stand guard over both piles, it'd be an even deal, wouldn't it?"

Abernathy spoke before Mercer could begin objecting. "That strikes me as being fair, Ben. Put the guns where nobody can get at them. It'd only be for a little while, until everybody's had a chance to cool down."

Mercer thought for a moment, then said dubiously, "Well, I don't think it'll work, but I guess there's no harm in trying." He added quickly, "Provided you can get the sodbusters to do the same thing."

"Tell you what," Foxx suggested. "We'll go back and talk to 'em, while you're talking things over with the men here. Then if everything works out, both of you can get together and finish settling the fine points. How does that strike you?"

Mercer nodded. "It's as fair a way as any. Go ahead. I'll see what the boys say."

"Good enough," Foxx replied. "And if we can keep things quieted down for a while, then we can start trying to find out who killed the marshal. Once we get the air cleared, maybe you and the folks from Sherman will see it ain't too hard to get along together without fighting all the time."

"It'd be a relief to have things quiet, so we can

work," Mercer said. "Go on and see what you can do with the sodbusters. We'll match whatever they do."

As Foxx and Abernathy walked back toward the houses, the lawyer asked, "What'll you do if they don't go along with your scheme, Foxx?"

"That's something I still got to figure out. It's just like any gamble, either it works or it don't."

"You said something about finding out who killed Ed Parsons. That's a pretty good-sized gamble, too, isn't it?"

"Maybe. Just remember, Abernathy, it's my job to find out things like that."

"So it is. Well, it looks like an impossible job to me, but I've been surprised before."

They were close enough to the houses now to hear loud voices coming from behind Fleet's soddie. Foxx said, "From the way it sounds, I might not be wearing this marshal's badge much longer. Not that it'd hurt my feelings to give it up, provided it goes to somebody who's able to handle the job."

"For the time being, you'd better hang on to it," the lawyer advised. "Unless the men elect a new marshal, which might be what they're doing right now."

Abernathy's hunch proved prophetic. No sooner had he and Foxx rounded the corner of the soddie than Fleet and Tate left the group of homesteaders and came to meet them. Tate held his hand out.

"We'll take that badge now, Foxx. We've picked out our own man to be the new marshal," he announced.

"That suits me fine," Foxx replied, unpinning the badge. "I didn't ask for the job, you'll recall. It's your town, and you men oughta have the say about who wears the badge."

"Who'd you elect?" Abernathy asked.

"Clint Burgin," Fleet answered.

"Burgin?" Abernathy frowned. "I don't seem to remember him, and I think I've met most of the men in Sherman."

"Clint ain't been here long," Tate said. "But he's been a deputy sheriff a couple of times, up north in the cow country. He'll handle things the way we want."

"Even if it's not the best way?" Abernathy asked, his voice expressing his doubts.

"Regardless," Tate snapped. "He'll make them damn grubbers over in the diggings toe the line. Parsons was all right, I guess, but he wasn't tough enough."

"You figure Burgin's tough, then?" Foxx asked.

"He might look like a dude, but he's hard as a keg of nails," Tate replied confidently. He turned and called, "Clint! Come over and git your badge!"

Two men emerged from the cluster of homesteaders and started toward the spot where Foxx and the other three were standing. Foxx recognized one of them as Frank Morse, the reporter. The other he assumed was Burgin, and seeing him confirmed Foxx's first suspicions. The new marshal was the man he'd noticed earlier, and mentally had tagged as a gunfighter.

Burgin kept a step ahead of Morse. Foxx noted the bulge of a revolver at the beltline of his frock coat and his opinion of the man dropped a notch. Foxx had never known a top-rated lawman—or gunfighter, for that matter—who'd worn his weapon high on his right hip. Morse stopped a pace or so apart from the group, but Burgin pushed between Tate and Fleet. He looked first at Abernathy, then stared at Foxx.

"You're Foxx," he said. "C&K Railroad. Well, you can go back to railroading, now that the town's got somebody who knows how to handle the marshal's job."

"I didn't ask to be made marshal, Burgin," Foxx said quietly. "I was just handy when they needed a man to fill in. I hear somebody say you'd been a deputy someplace up in one of the Territories, before you showed up here. Wyoming, was it? Or Montana?"

"Both of 'em," Burgin replied. "Long enough to know what I'm doing, if that's what you're getting at."

"Oh, I wasn't getting at anything special. Just a mite curious."

Foxx had managed to get a closer look at Burgin's boots than he'd been able to earlier. He noticed that they didn't have the stirrup-crease that marked the boots of a man used to spending a good part of his time on horseback.

Abernathy began, "Foxx has probably had—"

Anticipating what the lawyer was getting ready to say, Foxx cut him off, saying quickly, "You won't get any argument from me over who wears the marshal's badge. I'm glad to be rid of it."

Burgin smiled coldly, then looked at Abernathy. He said, "I hear you're the lawyer that's been helping those rowdies out in the diggings try to tear up the town. Well, I'll put a stop to that right fast."

Foxx put a hand on Abernathy's arm to still the

angry retort that he saw the lawyer was about to make.

Tate said, "I already told 'em we elected you to be the marshal, Clint." He handed Burgin the badge. "Now, go ahead and take charge of things."

"Before you get too previous, maybe you better listen to what me and Abernathy's just worked out with the prospectors," Foxx suggested.

"Well, I'll listen to you," Burgin said. "Even if it's not important. I've got my own ideas about what needs to be done here."

"Oh, I'm sure you have," Foxx replied. "But those men out there are ready to get along, and it'd be a shame if they don't get a chance to try to."

"Foxx and I have worked out an agreement that'll stop the fighting, at least long enough to give both sides time to cool down," Abernathy added. He was obviously controlling his anger at Burgin's slurring remark.

"All right," Burgin nodded. "Let's hear what kind of deal you've made."

"We've got the prospectors to agree they'll put their guns out in the middle of that space between town and the diggings," Foxx said. "Providing the men in town are willing to do the same thing. And I'll get a couple of men from the C&K construction gang to stand guard over both stacks until everything's settled down."

"Like hell we'll put our guns out there where any son of a bitch and his brother can get to 'em!" Tate exploded.

"Yeah," Fleet agreed. "I aim to keep my guns handy, too."

So far, Frank Morse had been a silent spectator.

Now the reporter said, "That sounds like a reasonable arrangement. It'd certainly put a stop to the fighting."

"Of course it's a fair arrangement," Abernathy said. "There's been a man killed, and I don't know how many hurt, so far. If things get much worse, somebody's going to get word up to Fort Hays that there's a riot going on here, and then there'll be troops sent to take charge of the town." Ignoring Burgin, he appealed to Fleet and Tate. "Is that what you want to see happen?"

"We sure don't want no bluebellies coming in here," Fleet said. "I had all I wanted of fightin' them during the war."

"Now, damn it, Fleet, there ain't nothing wrong with the Grand Old Army!" Tate snapped. "Happens I was one of them bluebellies myself, not too long ago."

"You two stop arguing right now!" Burgin told them. "The war's been over a long time, so forget it. We're all on the same side now." His eyes flicked to one side, where Morse stood, as he went on, "I can see what Foxx and Abernathy had in mind. Matter of fact, I was thinking about something like that, myself."

"Then maybe we made a mistake picking you out as marshal," Tate said. "We want somebody who's on our side, damn it!"

"You know whose side I'm on," Burgin replied. "But it'll do everybody good to take time to cool down."

Fleet asked, "You mean you're going to go through with that crazy scheme these two cooked up?"

"It might not be so crazy, if you think about it

a minute," Burgin retorted. "Except that I'd put a time limit on how long we'd leave the guns out there."

"How much of a time limit?" Tate asked.

"Overnight," Burgin said promptly. "And I'd improve on Foxx's scheme. I'd want one of our own men on guard along with the ones from the railroad crew."

"And one man from the diggings, too," Abernathy said thoughtfully, "I think the prospectors would accept that, Burgin. You intend to do it, then?"

"I don't see that it'd do any harm. You and Foxx are right about one thing. We need a little time to let the town settle down. And I need that to get my feet on the ground."

Hiding his surprise at Burgin's unexpected show of cooperation, Foxx said, "That's about how me and Abernathy figured it, Burgin." Turning to Tate and Fleet, he asked, "Now that your new marshal says he's satisfied, how about you and your friends? You going along with him?"

Before either of them could answer, Burgin said smoothly, "I'm sure they will, Foxx, after I lay the deal out for them."

"I'll leave that up to you," Foxx told him. To give himself a moment to think, he dug out a stogie and lighted it. "If you want me and Abernathy to go out and talk to the men at the diggings after you've got things settled on this side, we'll do that. And I'll take care of the two men from the track crew. But from there on out, Burgin, I'll be damned glad to tend to my own business and leave the town's troubles in your lap."

"I'm glad you feel that way," Burgin replied, stroking his upcurled moustache with a satisfied grin. "But I'll take you up on your offer. The men from the diggings are used to talking to you. It'll make my job a little easier."

"That's fine," Foxx said. "You get your men in line, and we'll go out with you while you talk to the men in the diggings. And as soon as that's done, I'll be glad to bid you good-bye. I already missed my dinner by mixing into this mess out here, and I'd just as soon be back in town in time for supper."

By nine o'clock, The Union had begun to get crowded. Men were lined up three deep at the bar, keeping Bert constantly on the move. The chairs at all the tables were occupied; the gambling tables under the balcony had a full complement of players and Sing, the young Chinese boy who did odd jobs around the saloon, had been put by Bert to serving drinks at the tables.

Following the agreement for the twenty-four hour truce in mid-afternoon, Abernathy had remained at the diggings to confer with his prospector clients. Foxx had stopped at the bar only long enough to answer Bert's questions about the fracas between the homesteaders and prospectors and to have a long-deferred drink.

After finishing his drink, Foxx had occupied the remaining time before supper by getting rid of the dust of travel and the sweat of his exertions during the day's inconclusive standoff at the diggings with a long, satisfying soak in a tub of hot water, followed by a change of clothing. A roast beef dinner at Mrs. O'Shea's had completed his restoration.

Now Foxx was standing with Frank Morse at the

rear corner of the bar, under the balcony, puffing one of his stubby, twisted stogies between sips of a drink. He told the reporter, "Judging from this crowd, every man in Sherman's taking the evening off to swap stories about the fight at the diggings."

"Everybody except the new marshal," Morse replied. "He's conspicuou by his absence, I'd say."

"I been watching for Burgin, too. Maybe he's staying out by the diggings to keep an eye on things."

"You're giving him a lot of credit, Foxx."

"Hell, I don't know the man. I got to admit, I don't cotton to his looks, but I stopped trying to go by looks a long time ago."

Bert finished serving the last of the men who'd been pounding on the bar for attention and came down to stand by Foxx and Morse. "This is the biggest night I've had since the gold strike," the barkeep said, mopping the sweat from his forehead. "You must've had a high old time out there today."

"It wasn't what you'd call fun. I'd just as soon have been someplace else," Foxx said.

"I'll have to agree with Foxx," Morse told Bert. He indicated the men lined up along the bar. "These fellows don't know yet how light they got off. Outside of the marshal and his deputy, there wasn't anyone badly hurt, and the men from the diggings were just about as lucky."

"I guess they're blowing off steam, too," Bert said. "One of them sneaked up to the back door right after dark. He said the new marshal had ordered them not to come into town, and bought a case of whiskey to take out there."

"That won't last long, as many as there are out there now," Morse commented. He yawned. "Bert,

I'm tired. I think I'll just take one of your rooms instead of riding ten miles to get home. I ought to be on hand early tomorrow, anyhow."

"Sure. How about the one on the end, Number Eight?"

"Fine. I'll see you men tomorrow."

When Morse had gone, Foxx asked Bert, "What about that Burgin fellow? Has he spent much time around here before now?"

"Not as far as I know. If he has, he didn't spend any of it in The Union. Hell, judging from how I've heard him described, I don't think I ever saw him. It wouldn't hurt my feelings a bit if he was to walk in the door right now, though."

"Somebody getting outa hand that you figure you're going to need help to handle?"

"No. I can usually take care of troublemakers myself. If they get too ornery, I've got a pickax handle under the bar, and a sawed-off shotgun if things get beyond that."

"You just want to get a look at him, then?"

Bert shook his head and a frown grew on his face. "I don't give a damn what he looks like, Foxx. What bothers me is that some of these fellows have had enough red-eye to start talking wild. They didn't get all the fight out of their systems today."

"Send your Chinese boy for Burgin, then. It's his job to sit on the lid now."

"I did that, just before you came in, when the ugly talk got started. He couldn't find him."

"What ugly talk, Bert? I ain't been listening too close, but I don't recall hearing anything but regular saloon chatter."

"It's mostly over at the tables. That one in particular."

Foxx looked at the table the barkeep pointed to. He recognized three of the four men sitting at it. He had no trouble remembering the name of one of them; it was Tate, the man who'd been especially hostile that afternoon. The faces of two of the others were familiar, and Foxx put names to them after a moment of concentration. They were Bob and Walt, the two who'd clashed with Parsons just before the marshal's death. They were bending forward over the table, their heads together, and just as Foxx glanced at them, Tate pounded the tabletop with his fists. The others laughed boisterously.

"I know all but one of 'em," he told Bert. "They didn't like it a bit today, when that truce was set up. They wanted to keep on fighting."

"They still do. Only they're not drunk enough to know that they've got no chance to fight the prospectors."

"Hell, let 'em fight each other, then. Kick 'em out in the street and tell 'em to have at it."

"I didn't want to bring it up as long as Frank was here, but they're talking about fighting somebody who can't fight back."

"Who, for instance?"

"Daisy, for one."

"Who the hell's Daisy?"

"She's one of the whores that works in the shack out back, across the alley. She—"

"I remember, now," Foxx broke in. "She's a water witch, too. The one that's supposed to've found the gold strike Mercer and his partner made."

"That's the one. I guess she's the only one they can think of to take their mad out on."

Foxx watched the men at the table for a moment, then turned back to Bert and said with a shrug, "Hell, Bert, they're pretty drunk right now. Chances are it's just liquor talking. Give 'em time to get a little drunker, and they'll most likely forget it."

"I hope so," Bert replied. "Not that I've got any special feeling about whores, but I get right mad when I hear three grown men talk about ganging up on a woman."

"I guess anybody would." Foxx drained his glass and shoved it away, took a final puff on his stogie and dropped the butt into the spittoon at his feet. He stretched. "It's me for bed, now, Bert. Been a right busy day. And I still ain't turned a hand to the job the C&K's paying me to do. Try to keep the noise down, will you? I'd like to have a quiet night's sleep."

Foxx had just hung his coat and shirt on the hook behind the door in his room and was pouring water from the pitcher into the washbowl when a light tap sounded on the door. He set down the pitcher and went to open it. The Chinese boy stood there, his eyes as wide as their narrow lids allowed them to be.

"What do you want, Sing?" Foxx asked.

"You, pliss, Mistla Foxx. Boss say you prease come click. He say there go to be bad tlouble!"

CHAPTER 10

Foxx put his shirt on again, not waiting to add collar and tie. He slid into his coat and vest and hurried back downstairs. Bert was serving drinks at the front end of the bar. Foxx glanced at the table where Tate and his cronies had been sitting; they were still there, still talking. Bert put down the bottle from which he'd been filling glasses along the bar and hurried to meet Foxx.

"I hate to bother you, Foxx, but you're the only one I could think of with the marshal not around," he apologized.

"I wasn't in bed. What's happened?"

"Nothing, yet. But right after you went upstairs, I took Sing's place serving the tables. I wanted to hear what Tate and his cronies were saying. They're mean drunk, Foxx. Hell, they didn't even notice it was me instead of Sing that was pouring their drinks."

"Well? What'd you hear?"

"Some nasty talk about grabbing Daisy out of the

whorehouse and taking her out to the edge of town. Gang-fucking her, then smearing her up with tar and feathers, and riding her around town on a rail."

Foxx said thoughtfully, "I don't imagine taking on three or four men thataway would be anything new to her, the business she's in."

"No. That's something Daisy's used to. It wouldn't bother her too much. But tarring and feathering's another thing, Foxx. I've seen that, back in Mississippi. Seen a man die from it. Hot tar took his hide off. It wasn't a pretty thing. I'd just as soon not like to think about it happening here, though. Not to Daisy or anybody else."

"Where do they figure to get the tar and feathers?"

"Why, Boyd's always got a big tarpot sitting out in back of his store. Half the houses in town have got leaky roofs. I guess they're counting on ripping up the pillows in the whorehouse to get the feathers."

"And you're looking to me to stop 'em?" Foxx asked.

"I've got no right to call on you, I know that. Maybe it's asking you to go out of your way too much."

"No. You did me a favor. I spent all day getting this damn town settled down. If those four yahoos bust loose, there'll be others join 'em. It could set off the whole town, maybe start the fighting again. Tate and his friends have got to be stopped."

Bert, frowning worriedly, said, "If you brace 'em in here, you'll have everybody in the place on you."

"Sure. I know that." Digging a stogie out of his pocket, Foxx nipped the end off of the stubby twisted cigar and lighted it. Through a cloud of pungent blue smoke, he told Bert, "Looks to me the thing to do is lay for 'em at the whorehouse."

"By yourself?" Bert asked. "Against four of them? That's pretty long odds, Foxx."

"Oh, four's not much worse'n one. Tate's the king-pin, from what you told me, and I faced him down once today."

"That was when he was sober," Bert pointed out.

"Sober or drunk, he don't bother me much. He strikes me as being more blow than go."

"I hear he can be tough. Don't let him surprise you."

"If I work things out right, Tate'll be the one that gets surprised."

"You're going to take on the job by yourself? If it was me, I'd get some help," Bert said, the worried frown that had been on his face deepening.

Foxx flicked his hand to indicate the barroom. "From this crowd? Hell, that'd be borrowing trouble before it starts. Ease your mind, Bert. I'll go out there to the whorehouse and get myself set. If they show up, I'll just play it like it lays."

"You know where it is?" Bert asked.

"I imagine I can find it easy enough. If it's like most of 'em, it'll be showing a red light."

"It is. Just go out the back door, you'll see it right across the alley."

Foxx started for the back door. Just as he opened it, Bert called, "Good luck to you!" Foxx nodded, and went outside.

Across the alley, just as the barkeep had said, a red lantern hanging beside the door of an unpainted frame house showed Foxx his destination. He crossed to the door; a hand-lettered sign was pinned to the

wall below the lantern: DON'T KNOCK, COME ON IN. Foxx
grinned, and went inside.

Foxx was not a man who visited bawdy houses in
search of pleasure; he'd never found that to be necessary. He'd been in a number of them in the course
of his job, though, and the instant he entered recognized the smell he'd always associated with such
establishments: a strong odor of carbolic acid overlaid with but not disguised by the aroma of cheap
perfume.

A tall kerosene lamp with a globular shade painted
blush-pink and overlaid with a design of garlanded
roses stood on a round table in the center of a long,
narrow room. The wallpaper repeated the design on
the lampshade, roses against a pink background. The
room was windowless, and on the wall opposite the
entrance there were four unpainted doors, all of them
closed.

Between the two center doors hung a chromo in
a glassless frame; the original legend had read "God
Bless Our Home," but the last word had been
scratched through and the word "House" substituted
in scrawled handwriting below it. Chairs in pairs
stood against the two end walls and a single chair
stood between each of the doors opposite the entrance. A push-bell was on the table, beside it a
small card bore the handwritten inscription, "Ring
the bell and sit down." Foxx obeyed the instructions.
He sat down and lighted a stogie.

His wait was not a long one. He'd barely had time
to get the twisted little cigar glowing good when
one of the center doors opened and a woman came
in.

She was amply proportioned, but big rather than

fat. Her hips were nearly as wide as the door, and her massive breasts, squeezed into an uplift by the tight-laced bodice of her dress, reached almost to her long chin. The tortoiseshell comb in the top of her high-coiled blond hair just missed brushing the door-jamb. Her face was in proportion to her body, a crag of a nose, high cheekbones, thick lips dark with rouge, and heavy eyebrows outlined with mascara.

"Evening, honey," she said to Foxx, a gold tooth gleaming through her wide smile. "You come to Madame Bertha's looking for a good time, I'll just bet."

"Not exactly. You'd be Madame Bertha, I guess?" The woman nodded and Foxx said, "Well, I'm looking for Daisy."

"That's what I mean, honey. Daisy'll show you as good a time as any of my girls. But she's busy right now. You'll have to wait a few minutes, unless you'd like for me to call Trixie."

"You don't get my meaning." Foxx stood up. "Daisy's in trouble. There's four ugly customers heading this way to roust her. Bert asked me to come over here and stop 'em."

"Wait a minute, mister! Just who in hell are you, busting in here and spinning some kind of wild yarn?"

"My name's Foxx. I—"

"Oh, shit, I know who you are now," Madame Bertha said, the frown clearing from her face. "You're the fellow from the C&K that was marshal for about ten minutes today, when the shooting was going on up by the diggings."

"That's right. And you'd better get a move on, because I don't know how long it's going to be until Tate and his cronies show up."

"Will you just stop hurrying me, until you tell me what all this is about? I know Tate, he's in here every week or so, most of the time when he's had a fight with his old woman. But the rest of what you're talking about just don't make good sense."

"Tate and three of his friends have been working on a mean drunk," Foxx explained. "They talked up a mad at Daisy because she witched the gold strike, and they're ready to give her a coat of tar and feathers. Bert heard 'em planning it, and sent me over here to help her."

"Why'd they be mad at Daisy? She was always nice to Tate, as far as I know. If she wasn't, it was because he's just naturally a worthless, hardcase son of a bitch."

"It'd take more time time than we got for me to go through the whole story," Foxx told the madam. "Why can't you just take my word there's going to be trouble, and let me get Daisy out of here? If I can get her away before Tate's bunch shows up, it might save your place from being wrecked."

Before Madame Bertha could reply, the door she'd come out of banged open. The madam's bulk hid the door from Foxx, and his hand went to his coat lapel, reaching for his House Colt. Then, when Madam Bertha turned and he saw the man framed in the doorway, his jaw dropped in surprise and he forgot about the gun.

He might have been looking at an apparition out of the past. The man in the doorway was lean and wizened, clad in fringed buckskin pants and jacket. A fluff of thin white hair haloed his head, and his bushy white beard reached the middle of his chest.

His nose was like a hawk's beak, his blue eyes bright and alert. In one liver-spotted hand he held a Walker Colt. The gun, Foxx guessed, was at least forty years old, and the man who flourished it twice that age.

"Damn it, Pete," Bertha snapped, "I told you to stay in my room! And put that gun away! You're too drunk to know what you're doing!"

"Drunk my lordly asshole!" the oldster snorted. "It takes more'n half a bottle of this horsepiss they call whiskey these days to get me drunk! Now, I heered this scallywag bad-mouthing you, Bertha. You say the word, I'll get rid of him for you!"

"If I want to get rid of him, I'll do it myself!" Bertha replied sharply. She turned to Foxx. "This is Santa Fe Pete. Don't let him upset you. We're old friends. He stops in to visit me every time he passes through town. But he won't give you any trouble."

"Not 'less you say the word, Bertha," Pete said. He slid the heavy revolver into a soft leather holster attached by thongs to the left side of his jacket. "I heard him say there was goin' to be some kind of a dustup. That's why I come to help."

"That's why I'm here, too," Foxx told the old fellow. He said to Bertha, "Except that you don't seem to believe me. Now, will you stop talking, and get Daisy out from wherever she's hiding? We haven't got too much more time to waste."

"All right," Bertha agreed. She looked at the old man. "Pete, you get back in my room. This ain't anything to concern you." After Pete had closed the door, she said to Foxx, "I still don't know what you're getting at, but maybe Daisy will."

She pushed past Foxx and tapped at one of the

doors. "Daisy!" she called, "there's a man in the parlor asking for you! Come out as soon as you can, honey!"

Bertha had delayed too long. The front door banged against the inside wall as it was shoved open, and Tate strode into the room, a pistol ready in his hand. Behind him came the three men with whom Foxx had seen him drinking at The Union. Tate swung his revolver to cover Foxx.

"Well, damned if it ain't Mr. Railroad Man hisself!" he grinned wolfishly. "Boys, it looks like we got two busybodies to learn a lesson to, instead of just one! Shorty, you look after the door. Bob, take the woman. Walt, see if Foxx has got him a gun yet. He didn't have out at the diggings today, but he might've put one on since."

Bob started somewhat hesitantly toward Bertha, eyeing her bulk. Tate held his revolver on Foxx while Walt stepped up and patted perfunctorily at Foxx's hips. When he felt no bulging holster on either side, he told Tate, "We don't have to worry about him. He ain't packing now, either."

"Well, you keep an eye on him," Tate ordered. He looked at Bob, who was closing gingerly on Bertha. "Damn it, Bob, I said for you to take care of that old bitch! I'll go find Daisy."

Daisy chose that moment to open the door. She stared for a moment at the crowded room, her look one of surprise, not apprehension. The noise of the door opening drew Tate's attention away from Foxx. He turned and took a step toward Daisy.

Foxx could see what Tate was going to do and moved the instant he was freed from the menace of the drawn revolver. Walt was standing between him and Tate, Bertha at one side. Foxx shouldered Walt, sending him careening into Bob, who staggered and bumped into Bertha. In the same motion, Foxx slid the House Colt out of the holster-pocket sewn inside his coat lapel.

Foxx's thumb was on the Colt's hammer as his hand closed on its butt. He had the hammer drawn back to full-cock and the muzzle aimed at Tate while Tate was still turning back to see what the sudden scuffling noise was about.

Tate had let his gun-hand drop to his side after Walt's report that Foxx was unarmed. The slug from the House Colt tore through Tate's chest before he could level his own gun at Foxx. He slid to the floor, his legs buckling, and was dead before his knees touched the carpet.

Foxx swiveled to cover Walt and Bob, but saw that Bertha needed no help from him. She had wrapped one of her big arms around each man and was squeezing them to her massive body in an unbreakable double hug. Foxx continued his turn to put the man at the door under the Colt's threat, but Shorty's hands were already above his head.

"Don't shoot me!" he called to Foxx. "Look! You can see I ain't got a gun!"

A quick glance told Foxx the man wore no gun-belt, and he held his fire. The door of Bertha's room opened and Pete rushed out, the Walker Colt in his hand again. He swung the big revolver's muzzle from side to side, looking for a target. When he saw Tate sprawled on the floor, Shorty's hands raised in surrender, and Bertha immobilizing the other two men in a crushing bear hug, the old man snorted.

"Damn it, Bertha! Why in hell did you send me

outa here just when the fun was about to start?"

"Because I didn't know it was going to start just then, you old buzzard! But if you want to help, hold your gun on these two so I can let 'em go!"

"Well, let go, if you've had your fill of hugging 'em," Pete replied. "If either one of 'em moves, I'll blast a hole right through 'em!"

Bertha released the two men, who stood gasping and wheezing. Bob gasped, "You careless son of a bitch, Walt! You said Foxx didn't have a gun!"

Before Walt could answer, another woman pushed into the door to stand beside Daisy. She had a small nickle-plated revolver in her hand. Everyone in the room turned to stare at her. Foxx's eyes were blinking with surprise, his mouth open in surprise. The newcomer met the curious stares with a firmly set jaw and unblinking eyes.

Before the silence grew too thick, she said calmly, "I do wish that someone would tell me just what's going on here."

Foxx finally found his voice. It came out as an unbelieving gasp. "Romy?" He shook his head, the frown deepening, and went on, "Romy Dehon? How in the devil did you get in here?"

"Through the door, Foxx. Didn't you come in the same way?"

"Now, you know that ain't what I mean. What're you doing in this place, anyhow?"

"My job. Just like you are, too, I guess, except that this is the last place I expected to run into you. I thought you were in San Francisco."

"Hell, I thought you was in Chicago. Or did Allan Pinkerton fire you and you've gone into another line of work?"

"You didn't have to say that, Foxx. Just to set you straight, I'm still with the agency. But we'll catch up later on. You go ahead and finish your job."

Shaking his head in disbelief, Foxx turned to Pete, who was still holding his gun on the three invaders. "You keep your gun on 'em, Pete," he said. "I'll make sure none of 'em's got a gun. Then you can line 'em up against that wall by the door while we figure out what to do with 'em."

Foxx made a quick but thorough search of the three survivors. Walt and Shorty were weaponless, but from Bob's vest pocket he produced a .41 Williamson derringer. He tossed the snub-nosed little gun over to Bertha, who promptly tucked it into her capacious bosom. With the men in line against the wall and Pete watching them with his bright blue eyes squinted into a fearsome frown, Foxx turned to the woman who still stood beside Daisy, though both had moved into the room by this time.

"I guess you can put that peashooter away, Romy," he said. "I'll get things cleared up here in a minute or two. Then we can go someplace quiet and have us a good, long talk. If you feel like it, that is."

"You know I do, Foxx. And this certainly isn't the quietest spot I've been in since leaving Chicago."

Foxx's ears caught the sound of a doorknob grating. He located the door and raised his revolver to cover it. After the fast-moving surprises of the past few minutes, he had no intention of being caught off-guard again. The door swung open to reveal a yawning young woman, wearing a thin off-the-shoulder chemise. She stood there rubbing her eyes.

"Good God, Trixie!" Bertha snorted. "Don't tell me you slept right through this whole ruckus!"

"What ruckus?" Trixie yawned. She stopped rubbing her eyes and looked around the room. When she saw Tate's body, she gasped, her jaw dropped, and her eyes widened. In a small voice, she asked, "Is that man there dead?"

"He sure ain't just funning," Bertha told her. "If you ain't the damndest one! Sleep right on through a raid and a gunfight and come out only half-awake!"

"Well, I put in a long night last night," Trixie protested. "And I needed to sleep, because most every night lately there've been tricks waking me up at all hours. What happened, Bertha?"

"Whatever it was, it's all over now," Bertha answered. "Now go get decent, and I'll tell you all about it when you get back." To Foxx, Bertha said, "Well, mister, I don't know whose mess this is, but somebody's got to clean it up."

"Don't look at Trixie and me," Daisy said quickly. "I don't mind handling a man when he's alive, but I draw the line at touching a dead one."

"Don't worry," Bertha assured her. "I wouldn't ask my girls to mess around with a corpse."

"I don't guess there's any such thing as an undertaker here in town, is there?" Foxx asked.

Bertha shook her head. "The barber takes care of seeing folks buried."

"Hell, a dead man don't need a shave," Pete remarked. "He needs a six-foot-deep hole before he starts to stink."

"I reckon the right thing to do'd be to hand things over to the new marshal," Foxx told her, his voice thoughtful. "Only it looks like he's dropped down in a hole somewheres and pulled the top of it over him. You got any ideas?"

Santa Fe Pete took his eyes off the captives long enough to say over his shoulder, "These son of a bitches here begun all of this. Let them take care of the dirty work."

"Now, that's the best idea yet," Foxx agreed. He asked the madam, "Is that all right with you?"

"It's as good a way as any," Bertha nodded. "All I know is that I don't want a dead man laying in my parlor. A customer comes in, it's likely to throw him off."

"I'll herd 'em wherever you want me to with the corpse, Bertha," Pete volunteered. "You just say the word."

"Now, hold on!" Walt objected. "If you let this feisty old bastard take us outa here, he's liable to finish us off before we're halfway to wherever it is we're going!"

"Shut up!" Foxx snapped. "You'll do whatever we decide for you to." He turned back to Bertha. "You said something about Tate having a wife, didn't you?"

"He said he had, didn't he?" Bertha asked Daisy. She nodded. "Yes. But he didn't seem to have much use for her, the way he talked sometimes when I was staying with him."

"I guess we oughta send her his body, then," Foxx said. "It ain't our job to see to his burying, the way I look at it."

"It seems like that's a cold-blooded thing to do," Romy observed. "Not that it's any of my business."

"You got a better idea?" Foxx asked.

"No. I was just mentioning it."

"Well, we damned sure can't leave him where he is," Bertha said impatiently.

"Looks like his wife gets him, then," Foxx told her.

"All right, Pete," Bertha told the old man. "You take on the job of getting Tate's body delivered to his old lady. Then come on back here, and we'll finish that bottle we started."

Pete waggled his ancient Colt in front of the faces of the three prisoners. "You muckworms heard what the lady said. Pick up what's left of your friend and get moving."

"By God, the new marshal's going to hear about this," Bob whined as he and the others started across the room to Tate's body.

"You tell Burgin all about it, with my compliments," Foxx told them. "Just be sure you don't leave out how the fracas started. Because if Burgin comes looking for me tomorrow morning, I'm going to be knocking on your doors by noon!"

Under the prodding of Santa Fe Pete's pistol, the three men picked up the body and sidled it through the door. Foxx finally felt free to return his House Colt to its pocket-holster. The room was totally silent. At last Bertha broke the hush.

"I got the idea you two're old friends," she said, looking from Foxx to Romy. "And even if this place hasn't been doing much business for the last half hour, it's about time for the late night rush to start. So, if you don't mind leaving now—"

"Sure," Foxx told her. "And Daisy oughta be safe enough, so we can—"

Daisy broke in, "What do you mean, I'm safe? What's happening, Bertha? I don't understand. What is it I'm supposed to be safe from?"

"I'll tell you later, honey," Bertha promised. "Now, you go touch up your face and get ready, because it's about that time of the night." She turned to

Foxx and said, "You know me and my girls are real grateful to you, Foxx. As far as we're concerned, you and your friend weren't even here tonight. And if you ever need anything from us, anything at all, we'll remember we owe you."

"You don't owe me a thing, Bertha," Foxx said. "What Tate got, he had coming to him." He looked at Romy. "We might as well be on our way. Like Bertha said, the night's getting along, and you and me have got an awful lot of catching up to do."

CHAPTER 11

As Foxx closed the door of Madame Bertha's behind them and took Romy's arm to lead her across the alley to The Union, she suddenly stopped and looked at him. The red light from the lantern on the wall behind them gave her face an unearthly glow.

"You said we're going somewhere and talk, Foxx," she frowned. "Where, in this funny little primitive town?"

"Why—over there." Foxx pointed to the back door of The Union. "It's about the only place there is."

"But that's a saloon."

"Sure. What's wrong with that? Don't tell me you've joined the temperance movement or got awful bashful since the last time I saw you."

"Neither one, thank you. But unless saloons are broader-minded here than they are everywhere else, they won't let me in."

"I've got a room upstairs. We'll go up there, where

we can be private. Unless you've got a better place in mind."

"I'm afraid I haven't. I'm staying at a boarding-house, and I just managed to squeeze by the land-lady's inspection."

"That'd be Mrs. O'Shea's?"

"Yes. The first thing she did was to warn me that if she found a man in my room, she'd throw me out. And the place doesn't have any parlor, just a sort of entrance hall."

"I know. I eat there." Foxx frowned. "How come you wasn't at the supper table this evening?"

"I was. Very early, though. And I finished as quickly as I could, because I wanted to have time to talk to Daisy before she got too busy with her evening trade."

"Ever since you popped out of her room, I been wondering—" Foxx began, then stopped short and said, "I guess that can wait. Come along, Romy."

"If you're sure it's all right."

"Oh, the men'll probably think you're in the same trade that Daisy and Trixie follows. Does that bother you?"

"Of course not." Romy opened her purse and took out a dark-colored veil. She said as she adjusted it to cover her face, "If I let what people think bother me, I wouldn't still be working for Pinkerton's."

Romy took Foxx's arm and they started across the alley. As they walked, Foxx was very aware of her light, delicate perfume and the pressure of her hand.

Before he opened The Union's back door, he said, "I'll give you the key to my room, and you can go right on upstairs. I'll have to stop at the bar and tell Bert what happened, and get my bottle, so we can have a drink while we're talking. Unless you really have gone temperance, that is."

"A drink would be fine. I imagine you can use one, too. But I do hope you've got something besides bourbon. I still think it's a barbaric liquor."

"Well, that's what my bottle is, but I'll get you something you like. As I recall, your taste's for brandy."

"Your memory's very good, Foxx."

He took out his key and handed it to her. "Here. It's Room Five. If I remember, I left the lamp burning, so you won't have to fumble around lighting it. You go on up. I'll hurry my talk with Bert as much as I can."

There had been no shrinkage of the crowd in the saloon, Foxx saw when they stepped inside. He stopped at the rear corner of the bar. The laughter and loud talk suddenly diminished and heads turned as the customers watched Romy pick her way between the gaming tables and start up the stairs leading to the balcony. Foxx could tell to the second when Romy disappeared into his room by the way the men lost interest in the balcony and resumed their conversations. Bert took advantage of the lull to step down to where Foxx stood.

"Don't tell me you found her at Bertha's place," he said.

"I found her there, but she's not one of Bertha's girls. She's an old friend of mine from Chicago."

"I'd say you've got pretty good taste in friends, Foxx. Did Tate and his bunch ever show up?"

"Just a little while after I got there. If you don't

mind, I'd as lief wait till later to tell you the whole yarn, Bert. But Tate won't be around no longer, if that makes you feel better."

"I take it you had trouble, then?"

"Nothing I couldn't handle. Now, I'll tell you all about it later on. Oh—if that new marshal comes in, you might forget I'm up in my room. I'll talk to him tomorrow, if he's curious about what happened. Right now, I'd like to have my private bottle and a bottle of the best brandy you got on your backbar."

"I'm short of good brandy, Foxx, but I've got some mighty fine Martell's cognac from France."

"I'll have a bottle of it, then."

In a moment, Bert returned carrying the two bottles and glasses on a small tray. Foxx dug into his pocket, but the barkeep shook his head.

"On the house," Bert told him. "So is your next bottle. Now, go on up and visit with your lady friend. I'll make sure nobody bothers you."

At the door to his room, Foxx tapped lightly. Romy called, "Come in. It's not locked."

Foxx went in and closed and locked the door. Romy was standing in front of the dresser, using its fly-specked mirror as she took off her veil. He put the tray on the dresser. Romy looked at the cognac bottle and smiled.

"Where in the world did you dig up a bottle of Martell's, Foxx? I must say, you do very well by your visitors."

"I do the best I can."

"Except for your room," she added. "It's even worse than mine."

Foxx looked around the bare little room, furnished

only with a bed, a single straight chair, a washstand and a narrow bureau with the silver on its mirror pulling away in spots.

"I'd don't guess anybody'd mistake it for the Palmer House."

"No. We've both had jobs take us to worse places, though, haven't we?"

Foxx stood studying Romy. While they'd talked, she'd taken off her narrow-brimmed straw hat, and now stood in front of the room's single window, peering out. She pulled the shade down and turned around to face Foxx. She saw his intent face, and smiled.

"Well? Have I changed all that much?" she asked him.

"Not a bit. You look just the same as you did two years ago, when we worked on that job of running down them swindlers selling counterfeit C&K stock in Chicago."

Romy was very much the city woman in both appearance and mannerisms. With her hat removed, a few loose tendrils of thick, black hair, worn short in defiance of the current fashion, swirled around her brow. If her nose had not fitted her full face and dimpled chin, it could have been described as a pugtype. Her lips puckered into a softly rounded rosebud; they were full and vivid pink, but Foxx knew that when Romy was angry they could be drawn into a firmly compressed line.

She was tall, but svelte rather than thin. Her breasts swelled firmly under the *tailleur* coat of her beige suit. The skirt dropped straight to her ankles from swelling hips and a flat stomach. The white silk blouse that showed in the vee of her jacket was caught at the neck by a narrow scarf. She took a cigarette case from her jacket pocket and Foxx scratched a match on his bootsole and held it for her. She inhaled and blew out a puff of smoke.

"This is my first one since dinner," she told Foxx. "I don't dare light one at Mrs. O'Shea's table, and when I smoke in my room, I toss the butt out the window."

Foxx smiled. He lighted a stogie, and indicated the room's single chair. "It's the chair or the bed," he said. "This town don't run to deluxe accommodations like you're used to, Romy."

"I noticed that in the boardinghouse." She sat on the side of the bed and bounced experimentally. "This mattress is softer than mine. I think Mrs. O'Shea stuffed mine with pebbles. But I suppose I'm lucky to have a place to stay in a town this small."

"How'd you get here, anyhow?" Foxx asked from the dresser, where he was opening the bottle of cognac.

"With a lot of difficulty. I got off the Kansas Pacific at their railhead, a dreadful dusty place called Sheridan Station. But I guess you know more about railroad towns than I do. To shorten the story, I begged a ride to Dodge City with a teamster. Then I rented a buggy there and drove the rest of the way."

Foxx whistled. "That's quite some jaunt. Must be a big case you're on. Don't Pinkerton's mostly send men out when a case is in rough places like this one?"

"It's a government case, Foxx, and Uncle Sam was in a hurry." Romy took the glass of cognac Foxx handed her and passed it under her nose, savoring the liquor's bouquet. "They didn't have a man closer than Washington or New York." She paused to sip the cognac. "I don't know whether you've heard, but the Agency handles a lot of Federal jobs now. Even more than during the war, the old-timers in the office say."

"Have they hired any more women, or are you still the only one?" Foxx asked.

"Two more. You know, when Allan hired me, he wasn't really convinced that women fitted into detective work. But he's changed his mind, now that I've done just about as well as the men. Better, in some cases, if you'll forgive me for bragging."

"Well, I'll admit, I was sorta doubtful when they told me I was going to be working with you on that stock swindle." Foxx took a final puff at his stogie and tossed the butt into the spittoon that stood against the wall. "But I changed my mind. You did a real fine job."

"Thanks. I thought we both did pretty well. But what about you, Foxx? You're still chief of detectives for the C&K?"

"Yes. Same job. I've got quite a few hundred more miles of track and a bunch more stations to worry about. The C&K keeps on growing, like everything else does, I guess."

"And you're not married yet?"

"I feel just about like you do about getting married, Romy. It ain't for people in jobs like ours. Or have you changed your mind since you told me that?"

"Not a bit. A husband and home and babies never have struck me as being the best life a woman can have. It's too dull." She held her glass out and Foxx replenished it. "Of course, my family doesn't agree with me. But they never have."

"Funny, us running into each other in a little outa the way place like this," Foxx said, refilling his own glass and lighting a fresh stogie.

"But nice, isn't it?" Romy asked, looking at him reflectively. "You said we had some catching up to do, Foxx. I hope you meant what I think you did."

"That's one of the things I like about you, Romy." Foxx smiled. "You don't beat around the bush."

"Not when I want something. And in Chicago, there never was a time or a place. Two or three times, I tried to work things around so we could be together, but something always happened to spoil it." She smiled invitingly. "I kept waiting for you to grab me just for a quick kiss, but you never did."

"I'm not much of a one for quick kisses." Foxx stood up and moved to sit beside Romy on the bed. "But we don't have to be in any kind of hurry now."

Romy turned her face to Foxx and offered her lips. He met them with his, and her mouth opened to his exploring tongue. For a long-stretching moment they held the kiss, clinging together, her hand holding his head and pressing it to her. Romy's lips were alive, rippling under his. Then she sighed softly in her throat, and Foxx released his embrace.

"I don't know why we waited so long," she said, standing up. "But now that we've broken the ice . . ." She began unbuttoning her jacket. Foxx took it and draped it over the chair, dropped his own coat and vest on top of it. Romy took off her scarf and turned her back to him.

"You don't mind unbuttoning me, do you?" she asked.

Foxx worked at the tiny buttons that ran close-spaced down the back of her blouse, while Romy released the fastening of her skirt and stepped out of it. She let the blouse slide from her outstretched arms. Foxx had taken off his shirt, and Romy stepped up to him and unbuckled his belt, then began unfastening the buttons of his fly.

"You'll have to wait a minute, till I get my boots off," Foxx told her. The walrus-hide field boots into which he'd changed that afternoon slid off easily. He kicked them aside and stepped out of his trousers.

Romy had finished undressing. She stood naked, watching Foxx, her skin a soft, rich cream in the warm glow of the lamp. Her breasts jutted high and firm above her flat stomach, their rosettes pebbled by the cool night air, the tips in the center of each rosette protruding a darker pink. Her legs rose long and slim to her dark pubic brush, her navel an elongated dimple above it.

Her eyes were drawn to the bulging erection that showed plainly at the crotch of his linen singlet. Foxx stepped to the dresser to blow out the lamp.

"Not yet," Romy said. She reached out and began unbuttoning the singlet, then pulled it down over Foxx's narrow hips to let it drop to the floor. "I like to look at a man when he's hard and ready."

She stepped up to Foxx and fondled him, her fingers closing over the fleshy cylinder jutting from his groin.

"I like to hold a man this way, too," she added, emphasizing her words with a gentle squeeze.

Foxx did not reply. He had bent to kiss her breasts, taking their tips into his mouth, first one, then the other, caressing them with his lips and tongue.

Romy's hand tightened around him. She squeezed

and released him for a moment in a slow, deliberate rhythm before bringing him up and pressing herself hard against him, trapping him between their bodies, swaying from side to side. Foxx stiffened even more as he felt the rush of warmth from her yielding flesh flowing around him. He brought his mouth up from her breasts in small nips of his lips, up to her throat and to her waiting mouth in a prolonged, tongue-twining kiss.

Breathless, they broke the kiss at last. Romy stepped to the bed; Foxx blew out the lamp and followed her. The light from the saloon, creeping through the grimy glass of the transom above the door, gave enough light for Foxx to see Romy lying on the bed, her face a blur in the dimness, the dark tips of her breasts and the triangle between her hips accenting her whiteness.

He lay down beside her and her hand went at once to grasp his erection. She whispered, "I hope you're not in a hurry. If you are—"

"I'm not," Foxx interrupted. "There's not any need to rush, is there?"

"Not after you've discovered how nice waiting can be."

Romy leaned up on an elbow, and planted a string of quick kisses along Foxx's bare shoulder before gluing her lips to his and thrusting her tongue into his mouth. Foxx cupped a breast in one hand and sought the triangle between her thighs with the other. Romy's hand circled his erection and she resumed the rhythmic stroking that she'd begun during their first embrace.

Foxx's fingers were just beginning to explore the hot moistness between Romy's thighs when she broke

their kiss. She rubbed her face in the matted hair
on his chest, then her soft tongue left a cool trail
through the softer, thinner growth on his stomach
until her face reached his groin.

She rose to her knees to bend over him, the tips
of her breasts rubbing his arm as she moved. She
grasped his jutting shaft and rubbed it along her
cheek, across her lips, down her chin, and along the
yielding smooth skin of her neck before she twisted
her head to stroke her other cheek for a moment.

Foxx lifted his head from the pillow to look down
at Romy. His vision had adjusted now to the room's
dim light, and he could see the expression of rapture
that wreathed her face. Her eyes closed, Romy rubbed
his tip across her lips. He watched her tongue creep
out and felt its soft warmth moving along his shaft,
tracing its length from base to tip for a few moments.

Even before she devoted her attention to his tip,
rasping it softly with her tongue, Foxx felt himself
beginning to throb. After a moment, when she took
the tip into her mouth, his fingers between Romy's
thighs grew wet as he penetrated her and rubbed
them along the swollen edges of her second lips.

Romy held Foxx in her mouth for only a few moments. She raised her head and studied his face for
a moment, then asked, "Are you enjoying my kind
of waiting, Foxx?"

"You don't need to ask me that. But it's been sorta
one-sided up till now. Don't you want to enjoy it
a little bit more?"

"Of course I do, but I didn't want to have to beg
you."

Foxx did not reply in words, but by lifting Romy
bodily and swinging her over him until her thighs

straddled his shoulders. He lifted his head, his tongue slipping between the lips already swollen by the probing of his fingers, tasting the saltiness of her juices. He sought and found the tender button of sensation and stiffened his tongue to rub against it. Romy quivered, and Foxx felt her mouth close around him again, her tongue caressing him with increased intensity.

Minute by minute their ardor mounted, until Foxx began holding himself back and Romy's hips were beginning to undulate gently in Foxx's supporting hands. Suddenly Romy released him and rolled away from him.

"Not that I don't love what we're doing," she told Foxx breathlessly. "But you must be getting close, and I don't intend to miss having you inside me. I love that, too, Foxx."

"Are you ready now? Or do you want to wait some more?"

"Can you stay hard?"

"As long as I need to."

"Then, let's wait more conventionally this time, with a drink."

Foxx refilled their glasses and handed the one containing cognac to Romy. She took a sip, looking at him over the rim of the glass as he stood naked in front of her. She sighed and said, "I'm sorrier than ever that we never did find time back in Chicago. Didn't you ever see me looking at you and wondering how big you were, and how long, and when you were going to try to get me into bed with you?"

"Sure. But every time it looked like we were going to have time, something new happened on the case."

"If I'd ever seen you stripped, I'd've made the

time, somehow." She reached out a hand to fondle Foxx's erection. "I think I've waited long enough. I'm afraid if we wait too long you're going to lose that lovely hard."

"It'll stay up until you're ready. Don't worry about me."

"I'm being selfish, Foxx. It's me I'm worrying about." She drained her glass and put it on the floor. "The longer I keep looking at you, the itchier I get to have you in me."

"I won't keep you waiting. You look real inviting to me, too." Foxx swallowed the remainder of his whiskey. "Whenever you say the word, Romy."

Romy rolled over on the bed. "I'm saying the word right now." She spread her legs and raised them. "Come on and fuck me! Right now!"

Foxx needed no second invitation. He lay down beside Romy and began to kiss her breasts, then her lips. She thrust her tongue avidly into his mouth and grabbed him urgently, squirming to slip beneath him on the bed. Foxx lifted his body to let Romy position herself. He felt the roughness of her brush as her hand guided him to her crotch, and the pulsing wet heat that enveloped him when she'd placed his tip inside her.

He did not need her hoarse urgent whisper, "Now Foxx! God, can't you feel how hot I am? Go ahead, hurry!"

With a swift, hard thrust he buried himself into Romy's ready depths. He held his pelvis firmly against her for a full minute while she squirmed beneath him, struggling to raise her hips. He felt her legs lock around his waist, and withdrew almost fully, only to drive into her again, and then again.

Romy cried out. "Yes, yes, that's it, Foxx! Go on now, go deeper if you can!"

Foxx straightened up a bit and arched his back. He thrust once more and Romy gasped as he went still deeper. Foxx still felt fresh and strong. He thrust repeatedly in his new position, as Romy clasped her hands behind his neck and lifted herself off the bed until she was dangling beneath him, swaying from side to side as he drove in and out.

"Oh, this is wild, Foxx!" she cried. "I can't wait for you, but for God's sake, don't stop! Whatever I do, just keep going as long as you can!"

He felt Romy's body shuddering as she went into orgasm, and maintained the hard swift tempo of his driving strokes until a whispered scream burst from her clenched teeth. Her body shook, her head fell back on the pillow and he felt her legs releasing their grip on his waist.

Foxx still did not stop. He fell forward, pinning her beneath him, thrusting slower now, holding himself deeply within her at the end of each stroke, grinding hard against her with his pelvis while her body heaved and the stifled screams trailed off and her mouth opened as she gasped for breath.

When Romy's quivering breasts stopped heaving, Foxx sought her lips. She responded with her tongue, the air whistling through her distended nostrils. Foxx began plunging again, but at a slower tempo now, taking his time, allowing Romy to recover. He kept stroking until her eyes opened and she looked up and smiled at him, her head rolling from side to side.

"I had a good one. I guess you could tell that. And I'm going to have another one—with you this time."

"You don't have to hurry, Romy. I'm not. Not quite yet, anyhow."

Romy bent her knees and pressed a foot on each of Foxx's hips. Her new position spread her thighs even wider than they had been, and without her weight on him, Foxx moved more freely. She braced her feet, allowing her to roll her hips from side to side in rhythm with Foxx's thrusts. He began to speed the tempo of his lunges, and in a few moments felt himself building to a climax. Romy gyrated her hips faster. She clenched her lower lip between her teeth, her neck muscles tautened and her head arched back against the pillow.

Foxx was driving now. He pounded into her faster, not trying to control himself as he had before. Romy began to gasp, and Foxx felt himself tightening up. Romy grasped his shoulders, pushing back to give herself the leverage to raise her hips higher. Her body started trembling. Foxx speeded up. She opened her eyes long enough to look up at him.

"You're getting close, Foxx. I can tell. So am I. Hurry then. I'm almost ready, too!"

Now Foxx's body took over from his mind. He thrust wildly, madly, driving to his climax. His trembling grew to match Romy's, and when her hips started jerking uncontrollably his own spasm took him. He made a final climactic lunge and fell forward, hips still moving reflexively, as he jetted and drained while Romy's frantic gyrations peaked and faded and she lay still under Foxx's now inert body.

Slowly, they recovered. Romy sighed, and Foxx moved to leave her, but she wound her arms around his waist and held him to her.

"No. Stay inside me. Here. We'll turn over." Romy

rolled onto her side, her thigh still under Foxx, the other leg hooked over his hips. She kissed him gently. "It does me good to go to sleep with a man inside me, holding me. Do you mind if I nap a few minutes?"

"Not a bit. I might do the same thing."

"I won't sleep long," she promised.

"We ain't going anyplace tonight except this bed," Foxx told her. "Go ahead, Romy. Sleep as long as you want to."

CHAPTER 12

Foxx watched Romy for a few minutes after she'd fallen asleep, then dozed himself. He napped rather than sleeping soundly, dropping off for a short while, then rousing to full wakefulness before closing his eyes again. After the third or fourth short interval of sleep, he woke to find Romy gazing at him.

"I told you I wouldn't sleep long," she smiled. "I'm still drowsy, but a sip of cognac will wake me up."

Light from the saloon still trickled through the transom. Foxx got up and filled their glasses, and lay down beside Romy again. She reached down and patted his groin.

"Even when you're soft, you look good to me," she told Foxx.

"You know how to raise me again." He smiled.

"That's something I'll take a great deal of pleasure in doing, but not for a while. When we've finished our drinks." Romy took a swallow of cognac. "We don't have to do things in a rush, do we? I can't do anything more on my case tonight."

"I'm not in any hurry, either," Foxx told her. "That trouble at the whorehouse is finished and done with Tate dead. It never was a real part of my job, anyhow."

"We've been too busy for me to ask you before, Foxx. What kind of case are you here on?"

"It ain't a real case, Romy. I was sent to get construction started on that spur the C&K's pushing south. I guess you seen that dug-up area outside town. Somebody made a gold strike, and set off a rush. The claims are right in the path of the spur."

"But why did the C&K send you to handle something like that? It's not a detective's job."

"My job's whatever my chief says it is, Romy. And it was his idea I'd do better than another construction man. That damn gold strike's got this town split in two sides. It's close to a war. You seen that tonight."

"I'd heard that the prospectors and homesteaders are having some kind of feud, and that there was some fighting today before I got to town. I didn't know any of the details, of course. But that's your case, Foxx. I can't see any connection between it and mine."

"Yours must be something special, to get you inside that whorehouse. What in hell was you doing there, anyhow?"

"I thought I might get some information from Daisy. It's just as simple as that."

"How's she tied into the case you're on? Not that it's any of my affair, but you wouldn't blame me for asking, would you? All I know is that you said it was a Federal case. What's bothering the government in this backwater?"

"Land swindles that add up to thousands of acres. At least, that's what the Interior Department people say. And they suspect there might be some state officials mixed up in it. That's one of the things I've got to find out."

Foxx was suddenly alert. The C&K had received its share of public land from Kansas as a subsidy along the new spur—640 acres per mile. Keeping his voice casual, he asked, "Is it homestead land, or our railroad land you're looking into?"

"Homesteads. It doesn't have anything to do with your railroad, Foxx, if that's worrying you," she replied.

"Just guessing, but is it the old six-month buy-out scheme?"

Romy nodded. "And it's being worked the same old way. Somebody hires a man to file on one hundred twenty acres, or a family to file on two hundred forty acres, and as soon as they've put in their six-month qualifying time, buys the homestead from them for the minimum dollar twenty-five an acre."

"Hell, Romy, that's been going on for years all over the West. What's so special about it happening here?"

"There's nothing special about the swindle itself. But the Interior Department's worried about three things. One is that it involves Kansas officials, another is the scale of the scheme, and what bothers them most of all is that it's happening so close to the border between Kansas and the Indian Nation."

Foxx grinned. "You mean the old boundary dispute they've been wrangling about since Kansas got to be a state? I recall it gave our land agents trouble when they was getting right of way for the spur."

"If it was just a matter of rigged homestead filings or crooked officials, it'd be up to the state to settle. But a few years ago, the Interior people made damned fools of themselves by including a big piece of Texas land when they were surveying the Indian Nation border, and they're still trying to get Texas to let go of it. They can't afford another mix-up like that one."

"So the Interior Department passed the buck to Pinkerton, and you've wound up with it in your lap."

"Something like that," Romy agreed. "The swindle seems to be centered around Sherman. A man named Homer Ingersoll has been buying up the homesteads, the Interior people say. Have you run into him, Foxx? You've been here longer than I have."

"I've talked to him once or twice, that's all."

"Which is more than I've done," Romy said. "In the little time I've been here, all I've found out is that he's one of Daisy's best customers. That's why I went to talk to her."

"Come to think about it, Romy, the first time I run into Ingersoll, I heard him offer to buy out a homesteader. I didn't pay much mind to it, because I'm interested in the gold claims, not homesteads."

"It's a lead for me, though," Romy said. "If you've got any other ideas, Foxx—"

"Well, there's a lawyer named Abernathy working for the men that're waiting to file mining claims,"

Foxx told her. "And a reporter for the Topeka news-paper might know something. His name's Frank Morse."

"Foxx, you're a gold mine of leads yourself!" Romy exclaimed. Then, excitedly, she added, "You know, we can't exactly work together on this. Not the way we did in Chicago, but we can compare notes."

"Sure. Whatever helps you might turn out to be helping me. Besides, I'm all for anything that's going to keep us close together."

"We're not exactly far apart right now." Romy smiled.

She swallowed the last of the cognac and leaned over Foxx to drop the glass to the floor. Her breasts brushed across Foxx's chest and he began planting kisses on her bare shoulder. Romy's hand trailed down his side to explore his groin.

In Foxx's ear, she whispered, "but I can think of things that'll get us even closer together. Suppose I show you a few of them."

Foxx and Romy had exhausted themselves and most of the night before Romy reluctantly returned to the boardinghouse.

"I've got to keep up appearances," she told Foxx. "I want to be in my room when Mrs. O'Shea an-nounces breakfast. And I don't think this place we're in has room service."

"Or any other kind, except at the bar," Foxx smiled. "But I'll be on hand at breakfast, and we'll plot up what to do today."

"No. I'm going to go back to my room after break-fast and sleep until noon."

"Sounds like the best idea yet. I might just do

the same thing, Romy. We'll get together after dinner."

"This afternoon I've got to follow up the leads you've given me, Foxx. We'll have to wait until tonight," she smiled.

At the breakfast table, Foxx and Romy had been formally introduced by the landlady, and had sat straight-faced and formal across the table during the meal. Romy had left the table first, and after a few moments, Foxx had headed back to The Union. He was still wondering where Abernathy might have disappeared to.

Bert shook his head when Foxx asked him about the lawyer. "He hasn't been around since the two of you left to go out to the fighting at the diggings yesterday morning, Foxx."

"You're sure he didn't come in after you'd closed up last night?"

"I'm sure. We didn't close until damn near daylight, and when Sing went in to clean Abernathy's room this morning, he told me that the bed hadn't been used."

"He must've spent the night out at the diggings, then," Foxx frowned. "Bunked with one of his friends, maybe. I'll just walk out there and see if I run into him. I'm sorta curious to see how things're going there, anyway."

At the embankment separating the town from the diggings, Foxx found the two piles of weapons, those belonging to the prospectors and the other to the homesteaders, still safely under guard. None of the men on duty there had seen Abernathy, however. He climbed over the low wall to the diggings and, after a bit of questioning, located the claim worked by

Ben Mercer and Red Simpson. Both of them were busy shoveling, standing in the wide, waist-deep excavation they'd created.

"Turned up two more nuggets," Mercer boasted. "One late yesterday after the ruckus settled down, and one this morning early."

"Any size to 'em?" Foxx asked.

"Big enough. 'Course, we ain't found any as big as them in the first batch we dug," Mercer replied. "But the gold's here, all right. I tell you, Foxx, we'll be sitting on a rich strike if we can just locate the main lode!"

"With all the digging going on, it looks to me like somebody oughta hit it," Foxx observed. "If there's a main lode at all, that is."

"Oh, there's a lode, all right!" Simpson said confidently. "It's just a matter of time before one of us comes across it. I figure me and Ben got the best shot at finding it, too. We've turned up the most nuggets."

"That's right," Mercer agreed. "And the next most has come outa Todd Hunter's claim, just up the line there from ours."

"All we got to do is keep them damn sodbusters off our necks," Simpson said. "If the new marshal's a reasonable man, he oughta help us do that so we can keep working."

"Has he been on the job all night?" Foxx asked.

Mercer scratched his head. "Well, I seen him out there by the gun piles a little before dark yesterday, but he's made hisself awful scarce today."

"Who I'm really looking for is your lawyer friend," Foxx went on. "Was he around out here last night or this morning?"

"Not as I know about," Mercer replied. "If he comes out here, he usually stops by to say hello."

"Funny," Foxx frowned. "He ain't been in at the saloon since the fight yesterday, either."

"Well, he can't be far off," Simpson said. "If he stops by, we'll tell him you was asking. Now, I guess me and Ben better get back to work. You know how it is, Foxx."

"Sure. No digging, no nuggets. Well, good luck to you."

Foxx wandered aimlessly through the diggings for a while. It seemed to him the area where claims were being worked had expanded since his arrival in Sherman. The diggings had now pushed past the end of the embankment, and were creeping around the west edge of the town. If prospectors continued to arrive as they had been, Foxx thought, the town would soon become an island in the middle of a sea of small claims.

He'd described a narrow loop in the course of his walk, and soon found himself back at the center of the embankment. Grogan, the C&K construction foreman, had replaced one of the C&K guards at the weapons stacks. Foxx climbed over the barricade and went to talk to him.

"You haven't had any trouble with men trying to get you to give them back their guns, have you?" he asked the foreman after they'd exchanged greetings.

"There's been a few try it. But they've mostly been pretty good-natured when we tell 'em we can't."

"Well, you won't have much longer to stand sentry, Grogan. Another couple of hours, it'll be time to hand all these guns back to who they belong to."

"Oh, it hasn't been so bad, Mr. Foxx," Grogan said. "It sure beats ducking bullets, like we was yesterday about this time. I'm real glad we stayed outa it."

"There wasn't no call for you C&K men to get into it. It wasn't your fight."

"That's what I kept telling the boys," Grogan said. "But I did get sorta nervous when I seen that fellow jump over the bank and start our way. It looked like he was coming after us."

Foxx frowned. He didn't remember any of the homesteaders even trying to cross the barrier during the fight. He was sure that all the shooting had been along the barricade, except for the shot that had killed Parsons.

"When was that?" he asked Grogan. "As I recall the way things happened, there wasn't anybody around your place up at the railhead."

"That's right. Just that one fellow that started our way. I thought you might've sent him to get us to help out. You was out in the clear space there, with the marshal and that lawyer."

"But he never did come up to railhead?"

"No. Matter of fact, I lost sight of him. I was watching you and the others walking up to talk to the miners."

"Did you recognize him?" Foxx asked.

"I didn't know who he was at the time. But I saw what he was wearing, and spotted him later on. He's the fellow they elected to be the new marshal after Parsons got killed."

"You sure about that, Grogan?"

"Sure, I'm sure. Damn it, Mr. Foxx, there ain't

nobody else in town that wears that kind of flattop hat or a coat that's clear down to his knees." As an afterthought, Grogan added, "Well, the lawyer wears that kind of coat, I guess, but he was there with you and Parsons."

Foxx lighted a stogie to help him think. As the foreman had said, Clint Burgin was the only man he knew of in Sherman who wore a black Prince Albert coat and a flat-crowned hat. And, because Foxx had been standing beside Parsons when the fatal shot was fired, he had no way of knowing Burgin's where-abouts at that exact time.

Stepping away from Grogan to get a clear look at the diggings, Foxx made an eyeball estimate of the angle from which the shooters must have fired in order for the slug to angle through Parson's body from the right side of his chest to lodge where Granny Blossom's probe of the wound showed the bullet had stopped, in or near the marshal's heart.

Foxx saw several prospectors' shanties and tents in the general area from which the shot must have come. The shanties were crude and unfinished, little more than a few boards propped up to support a canvas fly-roof. However, there were enough of them strung out between the embankment and the spot where the killer must have hidden to have made it possible for him to reach a hiding place unseen, by dodging from one to the next. Almost any of the shanties or the tents would have provided conceal-ment for the few minutes the killer would have needed.

Turning back to Grogan, Foxx asked, "This fellow you spotted out in the diggings, did you see where he finally stopped?"

"No." The foreman frowned as he tried to remember. "I was watching you and the others out in front of the houses there, Mr. Foxx. I just seen this fellow outa the corner of my eye, like. He was ducking along. Hell, I don't blame him for that. If you remember, there was a lot of shooting going on right then."

"And I don't expect you seen him leave?"

Again the foreman shook his head. "After the marshal got shot, I didn't see anybody out in the diggings."

"That figures," Foxx nodded. "There wasn't nobody watching anything but what was happening right along where we are now, after Parsons was hit." A thought struck him and he asked the foreman, "You didn't say anything to your crew about what you seen, did you?"

"No. To tell you the truth, it slipped outa my mind until right now." A frown had been growing on Grogan's face since the beginning of Foxx's questions. He asked, "You got the idea that this fellow I seen is the one that done the shooting? Ain't that what you're getting at, Mr. Foxx?"

"Maybe. Maybe not. I'll tell you what, Grogan. Don't you say a word to nobody about seeing that fellow moving around in the diggings when the marshal got shot. You follow what I'm getting at?"

"I guess I do. You need to be real sure, ain't that it?"

"You hit it to a tee. What we've been talking about is just between you and me, for the time being."

"Whatever you say, Mr. Foxx. You can count on me being quiet as a clam."

"Good," Foxx said. He looked down the street. A few of the homesteaders were already making their way toward the diggings in anticipation of reclaiming their weapons. "Guess I'll stick around awhile. Looks like it's about time to hand the guns back over to everybody. Be interesting to see how the new marshal handles things."

Foxx sauntered over to the house at the corner of the street, leaned against the wall, and lighted a stogie. The homesteaders saw him when they reached the end of the street and stopped, one by one. Most of them recognized him from the previous day, and while a few of them nodded in a friendly enough fashion, the majority of them stood a little apart from him, forming groups of their own.

In the diggings, the prospectors noticed the groups of homesteaders and began trickling up to the embankment. Bit by bit the crowd on the town side of the earthen barrier grew, and so did the congregation of prospectors on the diggings side.

Foxx could tell that Burgin was approaching by the turning of heads and the mutter of talk that rose from the homesteaders who now formed an almost solid line that blocked the mouth of the street. Burgin pushed his way through the clump of men. He saw Foxx and stopped.

"Well, I wasn't expecting to see you here, Foxx. Thought you'd be busy at whatever job it is the railroad's paying you to look after."

"That's just what I'm doing, Burgin. Until you or somebody else settles this wrangle between the townsfolk and them men there in the diggings, there's not a lot I can do to get our spur moving again."

"Well, maybe it's a good thing you're here," Burgin said. "I looked around for you in town this morning, but couldn't find you. It'll save me looking for you again."

"I slept in this morning," Foxx replied. "What's on your mind, now you've run into me?"

"There was a man shot in town last night. You'll remember him, I imagine. His name was Tate. You had some hard words out here yesterday."

"Oh, I remember him all right. Who was it shot him?"

"That's what I wanted to ask you about."

Foxx, wise in the ways of questioning a suspect, knew better than to volunteer any information or to comment on Burgin's remark. He said curtly, "Ask away."

"That's what I'm doing, damn it, Foxx! I'm asking what you know about it!"

"What's give you the idea I know anything about it? Just because Tate and me swapped a few hot words? That's mighty thin ground for accusing a man of murder, Burgin."

"I'm not accusing you of anything. Not yet."

"It sure sounds to me like you are. And I don't appreciate it a damn bit," Foxx replied. He did not raise his voice, just let his words fall out flatly and coolly.

"Did you see Tate last night?" Burgin demanded.

"Why, sure. Him and some cronies of his was in The Union for a while when I was there." Then, sticking to the literal truth, Foxx added, "But I didn't see him leave. Tate and his friends was still sitting at one of the tables when I went up to go to bed."

"Did you run into Tate later on, then?" Burgin asked.

Foxx took what he quickly calculated would be a safe gamble. He replied, "If you mean did he come up to my room, the answer's no. I've told you there was some other fellows with him. Why don't you ask them where they went?"

"I have. And they say they don't remember."

"Well, I guess that settles it, then, don't it? I wish I could help you, but it's just like I said. Tate and some other fellows, two or three of 'em, was still sitting there drinking when I went up to go to bed."

Burgin glared at Foxx with angry frustration. Foxx could see that his gamble was paying off, that Burgin had overlooked the key question that an experienced lawman would have asked at once.

Foxx decided it was time to divert Burgin's attention to a new topic. He said, "Well, you got all these men waiting to get their guns back. You going to keep 'em standing around while you go on badgering me?"

"I still think you know more about Tate's killing than you're letting on," Burgin snapped. "I'll talk to you about it later, Foxx. Just stick around where I can find you."

"You know where I'm staying, and where I take my meals. Anytime you're ready, you won't have to look for me very hard."

With a final glare at Foxx, Burgin turned to the business of returning the impounded guns to their owners. The job went smoothly enough; tempers of both the homesteaders and the prospectors had cooled overnight. Foxx watched until most of the weapons had been returned, then, mulling over what Grogan had told him and Burgin's almost open accusation, walked slowly down Sherman's street to The Union.

Bert was behind the bar, doing the odd chores that a barkeep attends to during slack hours. Except for him and Foxx, the saloon was deserted; apparently the general blowout of the night before was not going to be repeated at once. Bert put aside the glass he'd been cleaning and moved up to where Foxx stood.

"I guess you've been out at the diggings?" Bert asked. Foxx nodded. "And how'd it go? Any trouble?"

"Not a bit. I'd guess they all got a bellyful yesterday."

"You saw Burgin out there, didn't you? He was in here asking about you a little while after you'd left."

"Questions about last night? I got the idea your memory wasn't working so good. Just like mine got lost when he begun asking me about it."

"You know damned well I didn't tell him anything, Foxx."

"I didn't worry about that a bit, Bert. And it was easy to tell from what Burgin asked me that he was fishing without no bait. But too many other people knows the whole story. If it leaks out, and Burgin gets wind of it, I'm up shit creek without a paddle."

"I sure as hell won't talk. Neither will Bertha or her girls. Or old Santa Fe Pete. Don't let it bother you, Foxx."

"There's only one thing bothers me." Foxx had been thinking of Ed Parsons' murder. "If push comes to shove, it wouldn't faze me to stand up man to man against Burgin. But he ain't that kind. And it don't make much difference how careful a man is, I don't know of any way he can keep some two-bit gunman from laying up in ambush and putting a bullet through his back."

CHAPTER 13

For a moment after Foxx delivered his sober pronouncement, Bert was silent. Then he asked, "You planning to do something about Burgin, then?"

Foxx shook his head. "Not right away. I got other fish to fry first. Burgin ain't the first one of his kind I've rubbed up against. I can keep my back covered."

"If I can help—" Bert began.

"Thanks. I'll let you know." Foxx took a stogie out of his pocket and lighted it.

Bert asked, "Are you drinking?"

Foxx started to say yes, but changed his mind. "I don't guess so. My bottle's up in my room, and I'm too lazy to walk up and get it."

"That's easy fixed. I told you last night the next one's on the house. Keep the bottle you've got up there, and I'll open you a fresh one that you can leave here at the bar."

"Since you put it that way, Bert, I'd be hard-pressed to say no to you." Foxx waited while Bert opened the bourbon and then took the bottle and a glass to a table close to the bar. He asked Bert, "You've had a look at Burgin, now. You recognize him from anyplace?"

Bert shook his head. "Never saw him before that I can recall. I've seen a lot like him, though." He hesitated before adding, "And I don't mind saying right out, I haven't got much use for his kind. He strike you the same way, Foxx?"

"Just about. I've seen my share of hungry gun-hands, too. I guess all we can do is wait and see what happens."

"We don't have much choice but to do that. But I'd feel a lot easier if poor old Ed Parsons was still wearing that marshal's badge. This Burgin fellow—"

Bert broke off as the back door opened and Santa Fe Pete came through the dimly lighted area beneath the balcony and up to the corner of the bar.

"Break me out a bottle of my regular hundred-proof, Bert," the old man said. "Me and Bertha finished the one I got yesterday afore we went to sleep last night. Damn it, I didn't even have a drop left for my eye-opener."

Foxx grinned. He recognized Pete as being one of the last of a vanishing breed, and he'd liked the oldster from the instant Pete had broken in on the scene at the whorehouse last night. He called, "Come have a drink with me while you're waiting, Pete."

"I jist don't mind if I do," Pete replied. He swaggered over to Foxx's table and sat down. "I ain't much good of a morning till I've had a little tot."

Picking up the freshly opened bottle of whiskey, he tilted it up and let the liquor gurgle down his throat for almost a full minute before he swallowed.

When he put the bottle back on the table, its level
had been lowered by an inch or more.

"Now, that'll pop a man's eyes open for sure,"
he snorted, wiping his whiskered lips with the back
of his hand. He winked at Foxx and went on. "We
sure give them yazzabos what fer last night, didn't
we, son?"

"We did that, Pete," Foxx agreed. He took out a
fresh stogie and lighted it. "That was a job I might
not've been able to finish by myself. Lucky you was
there to lend a hand."

"Why, shit! I ain't had so much fun since the
hogs et grandma!" Pete chuckled. "Sorta takes me
back to the old days. By God, Foxx, there was some
hairy sonsabitches around then!"

"So I've heard."

"A man had to be a real man to hold his own,
them days. It ain't like now, when folks goes runnin'
to the law ever time they git their tit in a wringer.
Why, damn it! A man had to be his own law back
then!"

"You've been around a long time, haven't you,
Pete?" Foxx asked.

"Longer'n most, I reckon. I wasn't but a tad just
past twelve when I run away from home, wanted to
fight the redskins. Did, too. Jined up with Dodge
and Henry to fight agin Black Hawk and the Sauks.
Now, that was a mean, dirty little war, Foxx! Kill or
get killed it was, from nip to tuck! And then after
that I was all over out here in the West, after I taken
up with the mountain men. Knowed Kit Carson,
Jed Smith, all of 'em."

Bert came over to the table carrying the bottle
Pete had ordered. He put the bottle on the table;

Pete looked up and dug into his pocket. He pulled out a handful of cartwheels and tossed two of them on the table.

"I'll be pulling out tomorrow or the next day, Bert," Pete told the barkeep. "You better have your order ready, or you'll miss out. Wouldn't want your customers going dry, now."

"I'll have it for you," Bert promised. "It'll be about the same as always." He turned to go back to the bar, then turned back to ask Pete, "What're you figuring on doing when the railroad spur's finished? It's sure going to pull your business down."

"How's that?" Foxx frowned.

"Why, I'm a teamster," Pete told him. "Thought everybody knowed that. Been teamstering ever since a goddamn Cheyenne taken a hunk outa my leg with his tommyhawk in thirty-seven. Made long hauls on the Santa Fe Trail for damn near forty years, till the Trail just sorta petered out after the war. Hell, that's why most folks call me Santa Fe Pete."

"Is Bert right, Pete?" Foxx asked. "Will the C&K really put you out of a job?"

"Shit, no! I'll just move on ahead of your stinkin' enjines and keep haulin' till they catch up with me again, and move on further and always be a jump ahead of you."

"We use teamsters on the C&K, Pete," Foxx said. "If you ever run out of a place to move to, you let me know. I'll see you get fixed up with a job."

"Well, now, I take that real kindly, Foxx. But don't you worry about this child. I been takin' care of myself a long time, and I aim to go right on doin' it."

"Keep it in mind, just in case," Foxx told him.

"If you need a job later on, go into any C&K depot and have the dispatcher send a wire to me in San Francisco."

"Don't hold your breath waitin' for me to do that," Pete grinned. "There's enough places railroads ain't never goin' to run into so I can keep busy, what time I got left."

Foxx nodded. Santa Fe Pete stood up and picked up his bottle.

"Well, I aim to sashay out to them gold diggings and give 'em a look-see. They hadn't made the strike when I was here the last trip. By God, if it looks good enough, I might even put my mules out to grass and jine them damn fool gold-grubbers myself!"

Pete walked out jauntily, his bottle tucked under one arm.

Bert said, "He's a real old-time ringtail, Pete is. I hope I've got as much ginger left in me as he has, if I live to be his age."

"Me, too." Foxx agreed. He stood up. "Bert, I'm going to take a little walk around town before dinner time. If Abernathy ain't out at the diggings, he's bound to be someplace here in town."

"You sound like you're worried about him." Bert frowned. "I wouldn't lose any sleep because he ain't turned up yet, Foxx. He can look out for hisself."

For a moment, Foxx debated telling Bert what he'd learned from Grogan, but decided against it. He said, "Oh, I know he's a grown man. But it just don't make sense, him dropping outa sight without there being a reason for it. And when I run into something that don't make sense, I got a bad habit of dogging at it until I find the answer."

Foxx's walk around town produced exercise but

no information. He stopped in at the store, using a need for matches as an excuse, but when he asked Boyd if Abernathy had been in, the storekeeper shook his head. He needed no excuse to drop into the barbershop that occupied a cramped hide-building between Mrs. O'Shea's and The Union, but his conversation with the barber while being shaved yielded nothing but a highly embroidered version of yesterday's confrontation between the homesteaders and the prospectors.

Supper time was near by the time Foxx left the barbershop, the smoke from a freshly lighted stogie warring with the aroma of the bay rum on his newly shaved cheeks. He decided that it wasn't too early to drop in at Mrs. O'Shea's, not just to eat, but to arrange with Romy for the evening of catching up she'd promised. The street was already deserted except for a loaded wagon creaking away from Boyd's store and one or two pedestrians hurrying home for their evening meal.

Foxx walked leisurely down the street to the boardinghouse and into the dining room. Except for Frank Morse, the table was empty.

"Foxx," Morse said. "Just the man I need to talk to. Sit down. We can talk while we eat."

"I thought you'd be gone by now," Foxx said. He sat down across from Morse and helped himself to pork chops and potatoes from the platters on the table. "Figured you'd have to get the story about the fight to your paper."

"I decided it could wait while I run down another story that I just ran into today," Morse answered. "That's what I wanted to see you for. I thought you might be able to tell me something about it."

Foxx delayed replying until he'd filled his coffee cup. Then he said casually, "Depends on what the story is."

"Murder. I heard out at the diggings today that a man named Tate was shot last night. I hear you and the new marshal swapped a few hard words about it at the diggings this afternoon before I got there."

"I imagine what you heard comes pretty close to being what happened," Foxx replied. "Burgin's got some fool idea about it because me and the man that was killed had a little dustup during the fighting out there yesterday. I told Burgin all there was to tell. He didn't seem to believe me, though."

"Do you think he's going to try to charge you with killing Tate?"

"I don't see how he can, Morse. Sure, me and Tate passed a few words, but anybody with the brains of a constipated jackass knows you don't shoot a stranger over a little argument like we had. It just don't make sense."

"It seems to me that Burgin's got a grudge against you," the reporter said thoughtfully. Then he asked, "Have you two met somewhere before?"

"Now, where'd you get that idea, Morse?"

"Your job must take you to a lot of places. It's funny that Burgin would just dislike you the minute he saw you, without any reason. It just occurred to me there might be a reason."

"Well, there ain't. I never seen the fellow before that I can recall. I didn't have any reason either, but I didn't like him any better'n he did me. Got still less use for him after what he said to me today."

Morse nodded. "I got the impression you two didn't exactly hit it off from the beginning."

"I am a mite curious about him." Foxx frowned. "It don't make sense, him pulling into town and all of a sudden he's picked to be the new marshal."

"That struck me as being odd, too," Morse said. "I distrust coincidences, Foxx."

"I was hoping you might've asked him a few questions, like where he come from and how he happened to light here."

"Oh, I did."

Foxx smiled. "The way you said that, I get the idea he wasn't real free with his answers."

"He wasn't. He talked about being a deputy sheriff in Wyoming and Montana, but when I tried to pin him down, he kept changing the subject."

"He didn't give you the names of any towns in them places, then? Names you could check up on?"

"Not one. If I had any sort of lead, I could check through my paper, but there's no way for me to check out all the towns in two Territories. Not quickly, anyhow." Voices in the hallway gave notice of the arrival of some of Mrs. O'Shea's other patrons. Morse pushed his plate back and stood up. "We'd better save any more talk until later. You'll be stopping in at The Union, I expect."

"There's not much of anyplace else, now, is there?"

"Not in Sherman," Morse agreed. "I'll see you there. Might even buy you a drink, Foxx."

"I'll take you up on that."

Foxx finished his meal while the newcomers settled down and started eating. His plate clear, he replenished his coffee cup and dug a stogie from his pocket. He was just lifting his foot to strike a match on his bootsole when he became aware of the angular figure of the landlady standing in the door that led to the kitchen. He looked up; Mrs. O'Shea was gazing at him with a disapproving frown.

"I wear the white ribbon, Mr. Foxx," she said sternly. "I will not allow liquor or tobacco to be used in my house. They are evil habits. If you've finished your meal, you will please step outside before you light your filthy weed."

"I didn't go to offend you, ma'am," Foxx said meekly. He stood up, his cigar still unlighted. "I don't suppose you'd mind if I lighted up outside on the porch?"

"As long as you don't indulge yourself in my presence," she replied, going back into the kitchen.

Foxx went out to the narrow porch and touched a match to the stubby, twisted cigar. He'd taken only a puff or two when a buggy pulled to a halt in front of the house. He glanced at the vehicle as its driver reined up, and managed to keep a straight face when he saw that Homer Ingersoll held the reins of the buggy and Romy Dehon was his passenger. Stepping off the porch, Foxx waited for them to alight.

"Mr. Foxx," Ingersoll said, handing Romy out of the buggy. "Have you met Mrs. Dehon? She's just arrived in Sherman."

"We were introduced at breakfast this morning," Romy told Ingersoll. She turned to nod at Foxx. Her back was toward Ingersoll, who could see only the impersonal nod and not the tiny flickering wink she gave. "How do you do, Mr. Foxx? I hope you spent a pleasant day?"

Foxx nodded noncommittally. "About as good as I expected."

"I've simply been fascinated by what Mr. Ingersoll's been showing me today," Romy said. "You see,

Mr. Foxx, my late husband left me a substantial amount of money, which I'm thinking of investing in farmland. Mr. Ingersoll has been kind enough to drive me around and advise me about the suitability of land hereabouts."

Foxx recognized Romy's remark as being designed to cue him in on the cover story she'd adopted to get access to Ingersoll, and played up to her. He asked, "And you've decided to buy some land here?"

"I'm certainly considering it," Romy replied. She turned to Ingersoll, who'd dropped the check-weight to the ground and came up to join them. "Oh, Mr. Ingersoll, I'm afraid I left my purse on the seat. If you'd be so kind—"

"Of course, Mrs. Dehon."

Ingersoll stepped back to the buggy, and Romy whispered to Foxx, "About ten. Don't lock your room, I'll just come right in." She turned back to Ingersoll and took her purse. "Thank you. Now, if you gentlemen will excuse me, I'll go and freshen up before dinner." As an afterthought, she said to Foxx, "You should get Mr. Ingersoll to tell you some of the things he's told me about the country around here. I'm sure you'd find them very interesting."

"Wonderful opportunities here for the wise investor, Foxx," Ingersoll said, his eyes following Romy as she disappeared into the house. "This is some of the best wheat land I've ever seen. It'll bring a more lasting return on your investment than gold."

"It will if you've got railroads to haul the crops." Foxx smiled. "No crop's worth much unless you got a way to get it to market."

"Of course, of course," Ingersoll agreed hastily. "I hope you're making progress in getting the C&K's

problems settled. We need that spur through here, Mr. Foxx."

"Well, the C&K needs it, too. That's why I'm here."

"Have you heard that those gold claims might not have any legal standing?" Ingersoll asked.

"Abernathy mentioned he's been hired by the prospectors to see where they stand with the law."

"Yes. I have lawyers in Topeka working on that, too. On the other side, of course. Now, if the C&K would join me in a suit against the prospectors, we might get a favorable decision a lot faster. That could clear the way for you to start construction on your tracks again."

"I'd have to see what the head office says to a proposition like that, Ingersoll."

"It would be worth your while to recommend it to them," Ingersoll suggested.

This was not the first bribe Foxx had been offered. He shook his head. "I don't swing all that much weight in something like this. I ain't so sure they'd be interested, either. The thing is, if there's gold ore and mining gear to be hauled, the C&K's as interested in hauling it as we are wheat. We sure don't want to do anything to get them miners down on us."

"Your railroad's playing both ends against the middle!" Ingersoll snorted. "Straddling! It's time you people decided which side you're on!"

"We ain't trying to choose sides!" Foxx said sharply. "We want a way to get our spur moving again without hurting anybody."

"That proves what I just said!" Ingersoll snapped. "I'm of the opinion that we've got to bring this thing to a head. Those damned vagabonds out in the diggings aren't just holding up progress for the railroad! They're hurting the whole town! Think it over, Foxx. If you make up your mind to do something, you know where to find me."

Foxx stood watching Ingersoll's back disappear through the boardinghouse door. Then he shrugged and started to The Union. Though Bert had lighted the big reflector lamps over the tables and below the balcony, there was only one table occupied. Frank Morse sat at it, a half-empty glass in front of him. The reporter waved an invitation; Foxx nodded and stopped at the bar.

"If you'll hand me my bottle, I'll go over and chin with Morse a minute. Looks like he's got something on his mind," he told Bert.

"Before you do, I better tell you what happened while you were at supper. Burgin came in and rented a room from me."

"Did he, now. Give any reason why he's moving in?"

Bert shook his head. "Just said he decided it'd be better for him to be in town. But I'm sure he knows you're staying here. I wondered if he's figuring on keeping an eye on you."

"He didn't ask about me, did he?"

"No. Anyhow, I put him in Number Seven. Next to Morse. He didn't ask who his neighbor'd be, and I didn't tell him."

"Well, he might've been telling you the truth. I wouldn't let it bother me."

"It won't. I just thought you'd like to know."

"I do. Thanks, Bert."

"I'll get your bottle, then." Bert took the market bottle of bourbon off the backbar shelf and handed it to Foxx along with a glass.

Foxx asked, "I don't guess you've heard anything about Abernathy?"

"No. Maybe you're right to be worrying about him, Foxx. I don't remember that he's ever been gone overnight without saying something to me. And this'll be two nights in a row, unless he shows up later."

"If he don't, I'll be out asking questions tomorrow," Foxx promised. He went over to the table where Morse sat.

Morse looked at the bottle in Foxx's hand. "I told you I'd buy the drinks."

"Save your money till my bottle's empty," Foxx said, tilting the bottle over his glass. He sipped the whiskey. After he'd let it trickle warmly down his throat, he told Morse, "You left too soon after dinner. Me and Ingersoll had quite a little talk a few minutes after you'd taken off."

"About anything in particular?"

"Mainly about the men out at the diggings. I guess you know there's a mix-up over whether them claims they're working's legal, if they're on land that's already been homesteaded?"

"Abernathy's told me that. He's trying to get the legal side of it cleared up, but I don't know how much progress he's making." Morse looked around the saloon. "Come to think of it, I haven't seen him for a day or two. He's usually in here in the evening after supper."

"Neither has anybody else. If he don't show up tomorrow, I aim to start looking for him. Or some signs of him."

"You make it sound serious." Morse frowned.

"It might be. Like we was saying at supper, there's some funny things going on here."

"They were going on before you got here, Foxx. I gave you a pretty broad hint of that, the first night you were in town."

"You told me I'd have to do some digging. Well, that's what I been trying to do, but I sure ain't hit pay dirt yet."

"From what you said a minute ago, you're getting close. Try doing your digging along the vein you've just opened up." Morse stood up, obviously ready to end the conversation.

"Wait a minute!" Foxx protested. "This is the same way you done me the other night. Looks to me like it's time for you to put up or shut up."

"Sorry, Foxx. That's all I can say. It'll come to you after a while. Now I'm going up to bed. I'll see you tomorrow."

Then, as he'd done before, Morse walked away from the table, not hurrying, but moving steadily toward the stairs without looking back. Foxx took the reporter's action as a signal that pressing any further for an explanation of the hint he'd dropped would be a waste of time.

Foxx sat staring at the reporter as he mounted the stairs to the balcony and let himself into his room. Then he poured himself a refill and lighted a stogie. He sat there sipping the whiskey and puffing on the stubby cigar while a handful of late evening customers trickled into the saloon. Then, when the time when Romy had said she'd arrive drew near, he went up to his own room and stretched out on the bed to wait.

CHAPTER 14

Foxx was aroused from the light doze into which he'd fallen when the door latch clicked with a small metallic cough and Romy slipped into the room.

"You're not very flattering," she said, closing the door. "I thought you'd be waiting for me so anxiously that I'd find you pacing the floor."

Though the dark veil she wore hid Romy's face, Foxx read the smile in her voice. He swung his legs off the bed and sat up as she loosened the veil, removed veil and hat with the same gesture and tossed them on the dresser. He stood up and bent to kiss her before helping her take off the cape that swathed her from neck to ankles.

Romy went on, "You know, I feel like a totally abandoned woman when I wear this outfit, the way people look at me. If I'd been totally naked the men in the saloon downstairs couldn't have stared at me any harder. You should've seen them."

"I did, last night," Foxx said. "They'd've looked a

lot longer if they'd been able to see that pretty face of yours, though."

He gazed at her admiringly. Romy was wearing a tunic-styled dress of a soft fawn-colored material. The dress was cut low at the neck and belted with a cord that caused the garment to cling and reveal the full-ness of her breasts and the smooth sweep of her hips below her narrow waist. Foxx trailed a line of kisses along her shoulders and was moving down to caress the vee between her breasts when she lifted his lips back to her own.

When they broke the kiss she said, "I'd like a drink before we fall into bed, Foxx. You know I can't keep even a bottle of wine in my room at Mrs. O'Shea's."

"Yes. I got a temperance lecture from her when I started to light a cigar after supper." Foxx released Romy and moved to the bureau to pour their drinks.

She added, "And I've been dying all evening to know what you said to Homer Ingersoll that made him so angry. He was furious all through dinner."

He asked her, "How'd you happen to get Ingersoll cornered, anyhow?"

"By mentioning money. I thought you'd picked that up from the clue I tossed you when I got out of the buggy. I met him at lunch—where were you, by the way?"

"Out at the diggings. I didn't get away until it was past time to make it to the boardinghouse by noon. That can wait till later, though. Go ahead and tell me about Ingersoll, now you've started."

Romy took the glass of cognac Foxx handed her and sat on the bed. She said, "I don't remember whether I told you the cover story I handed Mrs.

O'Shea, that I'm a widow with money to invest, thinking of buying farmland. I certainly wasn't about to mention Pinkerton's to her."

"You'd be sleeping in a tent if you had, I imagine. She don't strike me as being a suffragettist."

"I'm sure she's not. Well, when she introduced us at noon, she passed the story on to Ingersoll."

"I gather he swallowed the bait, the way he was acting."

"He didn't just swallow, he gulped. He perked up like he'd just had a shot of whiskey and started asking questions. I strung him out by sprinkling a few dollar signs into my story, enough of them to make him remember that he didn't have much to do after lunch and to offer to show me some land he'd be willing to sell."

"Did you find out anything worthwhile?"

"Enough to know that I'm not on a false trail. He didn't say anything outright to give himself away, but I knew what to look for, and I found it. It was easy to see where someone had just torn down homestead houses on the land he offered me."

"I hope he didn't tumble to you, Romy."

"You know me better than that, Foxx. You've seen my poor innocent widow act. It's the same one we used to nab the C&K stock swindlers, and it's worked since then on other cases."

"Looks like your case is pretty well along."

"It's moving faster than I'd hoped for, thanks to you."

"Maybe even faster than you think. From what I stumbled on to out at the diggings today, I'm pretty sure I can make a case against Clint Burgin for killing Parsons."

"Burgin? Why, Foxx? To get the job as marshal?"

"That was likely part of the reason. I tabbed Burgin for a hired gunman from the start, Romy. I couldn't tie him to the killing until today, though. And it still ain't good enough for a case. There's more behind it that I still got to dig up. Burgin's just the man in front. I got a pretty good idea who's back of him, and I'm looking to you to do part of the digging there."

"You've got to be talking about Ingersoll," Romy said.

"It didn't take much guessing, did it?"

"No. I hadn't thought of him in connection with the murder, though. Not until now."

"Me either. Not until we got to talking at the boardinghouse this evening."

"What on earth did you do to Ingersoll to get him so upset?"

"Not anything I'd planned. He let me know there'd be a bribe coming to me if I'd talk the railroad into helping him block the gold prospectors. Got mad when I turned him down."

"And he stayed mad all through dinner, gave me a quick good night and left. If I'd known I wasn't going to have to keep working on him another hour or two after we'd gotten through eating, I'd have arranged to be here earlier."

"Well, now that you're here—" Foxx began, but stopped short when a light but insistent tapping at the door interrupted him.

Romy dropped her voice and asked, "Were you expecting somebody, Foxx?"

He shook his head. The tapping was repeated. Foxx's coat was hanging over the back of the chair.

He reached inside the fold of its lapel and slid his House Colt from the sewn-in holster-pocket and drew back the hammer as he walked softly to the door.

Standing to one side of the door itself, where he'd be clear if someone put a shot through the panel, he asked, "Who is it?"

"Morse. I need to talk to you right now."

Foxx looked questioningly at Romy. She nodded. Foxx unlocked the door and opened it. Frank Morse started to come into the room, saw the gun in Foxx's hand and stepped back.

Foxx lowered the weapon. "It's all right, Morse. A man just never knows who's knocking, sometimes."

Now Morse noticed Romy for the first time. He drew back and said, "I'm sorry, Foxx. It didn't occur to me you might have company. I saw the light in your transom, and just—" Morse broke off in mid-sentence and looked closely at Romy, frowning. "Why —I've seen you at Mrs. O'Shea's."

Foxx said, "Come on in, Morse, so I can close the door." Morse entered, his eyes still fixed on Romy. After closing the door, Foxx told her, "This is the newspaper reporter I mentioned. Looks like we're going to have to trust him to keep his mouth shut."

"Will he?" she asked.

"He has so far, when I asked him to."

Romy nodded. "Go ahead and tell him, Foxx, if you think it's all right."

"What's going on here, Foxx?" Morse asked, looking from Foxx to Romy with a puzzled frown.

"This lady's Romy Dehon. She's a Pinkerton operative, outa Chicago, working on a land swindle scheme for the Federals."

"Well, thank God!" Morse said. He turned to Romy. "You're going to take a big load off my mind, Mrs. Dehon."

"How's that?" she asked.

"I'll tell you later." Morse turned back to Foxx. "Did you know that Clint Burgin's moved into the room next to mine?"

"Bert mentioned it to me. Why?"

"Because the walls between these damned rooms—excuse me, Mrs. Dehon—are just one board thick, and you can hear everything that's said in the room next to whichever one you're in. And right now, Burgin and Homer Ingersoll are in Burgin's room having a talk you ought to hear." Then, remembering Romy, added, "You, too, Mrs. Dehon."

"What're they talking about?" Foxx asked.

"You ought to hear it for yourself," Morse replied. "But if you're going to listen, you'll have to hurry."

"We'd better go, then, Foxx," Romy said. "Especially if it affects both our cases."

"Just walk quietly," Morse warned.

Foxx tucked the revolver in his pocket, then he and Romy followed Morse along the railed walkway that gave access to the rooms. It exposed them to the view of those on the saloon's main floor, but when Foxx looked down he saw no eyes watching the balcony. The door to Morse's room was open. Romy and Foxx followed him inside. When he closed the door, they could hear a low murmur of voices coming from the adjoining room.

Keeping his voice to a whisper, Morse said, "Press your ear to the wall. You can hear them plainly."

"Wait," Romy whispered.

She pointed to a tray holding a half-dozen glasses on the washstand. Tiptoeing to the stand, she brought back a glass for each of them.

Still whispering, she said, "Push the open end of the glass against the wall, and put your ear on the other end. It's like a doctor's stethoscope; you can hear a lot better."

When Foxx pressed his ear to the bottom of the glass, he found that he could hear the voices in the next room as clearly as if he'd been standing in there with Burgin and Ingersoll.

Burgin was saying, "It's all settled then, except for the pay. I'll find somebody to stir up some fresh trouble out at the diggings, then I'll deputize a posse to clear the prospectors out, every man jack of 'em."

"I want it done as soon as you can make your arrangements," Ingersoll said. "Those small mining claims could give me a great deal of trouble. If a judge rules they're legal, I stand to lose about four sections of valuable land. What's worse, they could tie my plans up for months, even for years."

"So you've said. It's too bad for you that first scheme of getting the sodbusters to run 'em out didn't work."

"It'd have worked if I'd had Parsons on my side, but he wouldn't listen to me. That's why I had Tate send for you. And I must say, he was right in recommending you. You delivered."

"Hell, Tate and me went back a long way," Burgin replied. "Too bad about him. If I'm right in my hunch, I've got a score to settle with Foxx for Tate."

"I'll miss Tate, too," Ingersoll said. "He had five homesteads claimed for me under different names. Now I've got to find somebody else to take them up or lose more than a thousand acres of good wheat-land."

"Well, Tate's gone," Burgin pointed out. "And I'm here ready to do whatever else you need. Outside of sitting on a hunk of bare prairie for six months. That's not my style."

"You know what I want done. How soon can you get together the men you'll need and give me some action?"

"It'll take a little time," Burgin replied. "Three or four days, maybe a week."

"Can't you work any faster?" Ingersoll asked.

"That depends. I can do most anything, if the pay's right."

"How much would you expect?"

After a short silence, Burgin said, "I'll need about ten men. They'll cost you, oh, hell, ten dollars a head for a job like that. And two hundred for me."

"That's as much as I paid you for taking care of Parsons!" Ingersoll protested. "And clearing those rascals out of the diggings can't be compared to that job!"

"Like hell it can't, Ingersoll! Those bastards have got guns! And they'll be ready to use 'em! I oughta charge you twice that and I would if it wasn't for that other job you said you want me to do: the lawyer, Abernathy."

"I didn't say I wasn't willing to pay you!" Ingersoll protested. "What I was getting at is that if I hire you for two more—ah—jobs, I should get a lower price."

"I'm damned if I'll give you one!" Burgin retorted.

"You're a businessman, Burgin. You know that's just simple business practice."

"Look here, Ingersoll, I let you off for two hundred on the Parsons job because Tate set the price. Now, I won't complain about that. It was a snap, just like he promised it'd be. But taking care of the lawyer won't be all that easy."

"I don't see why not. You told me yesterday how you operate. One man, one bullet, I think you said. Arrest him for anything you can think of, shoot him, and say he was trying to get away."

"If it's that easy, you don't need me, Ingersoll. Now, as near as I've found out, Abernathy ain't by hisself a lot. I hear he's taken to spending most of his time with that fellow Foxx from the railroad. I might wind up having to kill both of them."

"That wouldn't displease me," Ingersoll replied. "Foxx is like Parsons; I can't buy him, either. He could make trouble."

"If it turns out I do have to handle Foxx, it'll cost you extra," Burgin warned.

"How much extra?" Ingersoll asked.

Listening to him, Foxx could almost see Ingersoll's crow-beak nose quivering and his thin lips squeezing into a tight line. Burgin was apparently doing some mental arithmetic, for his response took a long time coming.

"I'll make you a bargain rate," Burgin said at last. "Five hundred over whatever it costs for the men I hire for the deal on getting rid of the prospectors and Abernathy, and nothing extra if I have to take Foxx, too. I'll throw him in free."

"I've already paid you two hundred for Parsons," Ingersoll objected. "You ought to give me back a hundred if you don't kill Foxx. Why should I pay extra for something you don't do?"

"Because I'm here, damn it, and ready to do the job! If you think you can get somebody else, go ahead! But if you're in a hurry for action, you can by God take my deal!"

There was another long silence in the adjoining room. Foxx figured that it must be Ingersoll thinking things over this time. Then Ingersoll spoke.

"You've got me over a barrel, Burgin. All right. It's a deal."

"Half in advance, half when I finish," Burgin told him.

"You didn't collect in advance for Parsons!"

"That was before I seen you, Ingersoll. Now I've got better acquainted, I want half the cash before I lift a finger. Tonight, if you're in as big a hurry as you make out to be."

"Don't insult me, Burgin!" Ingersoll snapped. "All I've got to do is drop the word to my Topeka connections, and you'll be taking a gallows walk!"

"I won't take it by myself. You'll swing on the rope next to me. Face up to it. We're in this together."

There was another moment of silence. Then Ingersoll said, "All right. But I don't carry that much money with me. I'll have it for you in the morning."

"Good. And I'll take care of the job just as fast as I can. If you want to know something, I can't get out of this damn burg any too fast to suit me."

"That's fine. The quicker, the better. I've got a silly little biddy of a city widow on the hook right now, but I don't have much hope that she'll take the bait as long as there's trouble in town."

A scraping of chair legs sounded in the room, followed by the snap of a door being unlocked. Then Burgin asked, "Where'll we meet to pass the money?"

"Downstairs is as good a place as any, I suppose. Mornings are a slack time in The Union. You be at a table toward the back, and I'll stop by to say hello. We can pick a time and pass the money when nobody's watching."

"Fair enough. I'll look for you, then."

There was the click of the door latch and the sound of it opening and closing. In Morse's room, the three looked from one to another until Foxx whispered, "Give Ingersoll time to get out of the saloon, and we'll go down to my room where we can talk without Burgin listening like we been doing."

They waited in strained silence until the thumping of boots being dropped to the floor, followed by the creaking of bedsprings, told them Burgin had settled in for the night. To be safe, they waited a few minutes longer to allow plenty of time for Ingersoll to get out of the saloon. Then, with Foxx leading, keeping as close as possible to the wall and away from the railing, they returned to his room.

When they were safely inside with the door closed, Foxx told them, "Well, there's one thing I heard tonight makes me feel considerable better, even if it does raise a brand-new question."

"What's that?" Romy said.

"Abernathy. He's been missing for two days now, and I was just about to go looking for fresh graves close to town. At least I know now that Burgin didn't kill him. Or hasn't yet, anyhow."

"What makes you so sure he hasn't?" Romy asked. "I've got a nasty suspicious streak, Foxx—you know that. Burgin may have shot him, and hadn't told Ingersoll. Now he'll produce your friend's body and collect his blood money."

"Not likely, Romy," Foxx replied promptly. "If Ingersoll don't see him do a killing, or hear about it right after it happened, he won't pay off. His kind's as stingy as they are ugly."

"What's happened to Abernathy, then?" Morse asked.

"Your guess on that's as good as mine," Foxx replied. "But I'll put up dollars against doughnuts he's kited off someplace to do something that popped into his mind, and just didn't stop to tell anybody what he was going to do."

"You're probably right," Romy said. "At least you've got the same opinion about Ingersoll that I have."

"We'll find out soon enough, I imagine," Foxx said. He turned to the reporter. "Anyhow, Morse, it looks like you got yourself a hell of a fine story for your newspaper."

Morse shook his head. "It's one I can't write. Not right away, at least."

"Why not?" Romy asked. "You heard them yourself."

"I heard something you two might not've been paying much attention to. I'm pretty sure the owner of the paper is one of the Topeka 'connections' that Ingersoll mentioned."

Foxx stared. "The hell you say!"

"Why do you think I've been dropping hints to you, Foxx, instead of just coming right out with plain language? Whenever I write about homestead land frauds and get too close to the bone, my stories don't get into print, or they get all the meaning edited out of them."

Romy said thoughtfully, "It happens, of course. Why don't you try another paper, Mr. Morse?"

"I would, if there was one. Or if I were a lot younger. I don't have a railroad behind me, or a big detective agency. I'm just one man by himself, juggling something that's too big and too hot for me to handle alone."

"Seems like a smart fellow like you'd figure out a way to handle it, Morse," Foxx frowned.

"I've tried to think of one, but I can't. I guess I'm not the bravest man in the world, Foxx. I want to stay alive, and I'm afraid that if I get too close to the heart of this mess, there'll be somebody like Burgin turned loose on me."

"You're probably right about that," Romy agreed. She turned to Foxx. "Well, between us, we ought to be able to help Mr. Morse, wouldn't you say?"

Foxx nodded. He told Morse, "You just sit tight for a day or so while me and Romy look and listen. If you run across anything new, let us know. I got a hunch this case is just about to bust wide open."

"If that's what you think is best." Morse looked from Foxx to Romy and went on, "I guess you'll want to make some plans now, so I'll leave you alone. If I can help—"

"We'll let you know," Foxx promised. Morse nodded his good nights and Foxx let him out. After locking the door, he turned to Romy and asked, "You feel like I do about what's happened?"

"If I didn't know better, I'd say it was Christmas." She sat down on the bed. "Don't you think we need a drink to celebrate, Foxx? It's not every day that

we get handed the solution to a case on a silver platter."

"It's not ended yet," Foxx cautioned her. "Burgin's
a hired killer. His kind don't warn you the way a
rattlesnake does. No, Romy. Burgin—he'd hit when
he sees you, like a copperhead."

"I know that," she said soberly, taking the glass
Foxx handed her. Then she chuckled and a grin
swept the sober expression off her face. "How does
it feel to be bargain basement merchandise, Foxx?
Burgin certainly doesn't value you very highly."

"Now, that ain't no way for a silly little biddy of
a city widow to be talking," Foxx grinned.

"I owe Ingersoll one for that," Romy smiled. "I'll
pay him back, too." She drained her glass and
stretched luxuriously. "I didn't come up here to
work on my case tonight, Foxx. I came up here to
forget about it. Don't you think it's time for us to
stop talking shop and pay some attention to our per-
sonal life?"

"I'd say it's way past time."

Foxx held out his hand. Romy took it and he
pulled her to her feet and into his arms. They clung
and kissed, Foxx rubbing her breasts with his hand
until he felt her nipples bud and grow firm. Romy's
hand crept to Foxx's crotch and fumbled buttons
loose until she could slip it inside and close her fingers around him.

Foxx began to grow hard. He found the knot of
the cord that belted her dress and pulled it free.
Romy twisted her body and shrugged. The dress and
the light shift that was under it rippled down her
body, leaving her standing naked except for her
pumps and stockings.

"You see, I came prepared tonight," she whispered.

Foxx did not answer, his lips were busy roaming her body, stopping now and then to close over the puckered rosettes of her breasts. Romy freed his erection and caressed her pubic brush with his tip before tucking him between her thighs and pressing them together to entrap him.

"You've got too many clothes on, Foxx," she suggested after a moment. "I'm more than ready. And from what I feel between my legs, you are, too."

She stepped back and sat on the bed. Foxx slipped out of his boots and began taking off his trousers. When he'd finished undressing, he bent over the dresser and blew out the lamp.

"We'd've started a lot sooner if I'd had sense enough to put this out before Morse came knocking." He stretched out beside Romy on the bed. "But without that light showing through the transom, anybody else that comes looking for me is going to think I'm gone and leave without knocking."

"I don't begrudge the time we lost." Romy breathed. Her hands were busy roaming over Foxx's body. "At least, not much. And not now."

Foxx reached out a hand to caress her, but Romy was already kneeling on the bed beside him. He said, "Neither one of us does, I guess."

Romy did not answer, but Foxx had not expected her to.

CHAPTER 15

Foxx sat in the uncomfortably straight chair in his room, one boot on, the other in his hands. An unlighted stogie was clenched between his straight white teeth, an untouched drink sat on the dresser at his elbow. The first hint of pre-dawn gray was beginning to show at the bottom of the window where the shade lacked an inch of meeting the sill.

Romy had left a little more than an hour ago to return to the boardinghouse before daylight. Foxx had lain back on the bed, wrapped in the warm muskiness of her perfume, ready to go to sleep. Before he'd dozed, though, he'd started thinking about the events of the evening, and from there it was a short step to project his thoughts into the future and begin to form plans.

Once his mind became engrossed in planning, sleep had become impossible. He'd sat on the side of the bed while he smoked a stogie and sipped a glass of bourbon, but when he lay down again, sleep was as faraway as ever. He tossed restlessly until the hint of false dawn showed in the gap below the window shade, and by that time his stomach had begun to demand attention.

His gold half-hunter watch lay on the dresser; Foxx pressed the repeater lever and the watch responded with four muted musical tinkles that told him that he still had a long, hungry hour to wait before Pancake Jack's would be open for business. Resigning himself to the belly-gripes that lay ahead, Foxx got up, poured a fresh drink, and took out another stogie before he started dressing.

Pulling on his other boot, Foxx stood up and lighted the lamp and his stogie with the same match. For the first time since arriving in Sherman, he lifted his American Model Smith & Wesson out of the dresser drawer and drew the long-barreled gun from its holster. Opening his valise, he took out the boxes of fresh .38 and .41 cartridges and the flat, flannel-wrapped can of gun oil that were always in his travel kit.

While the strip of light below the window shade grew steadily brighter, Foxx broke the gun and upended the barrel. The five shells in the cylinder dropped into his hand. Foxx laid them on the dresser and squinted at the lamp flame through the top chamber to inspect the bore. It showed clean and shining, no traces of dirt on the lands.

He squeezed a drop of oil into the action and on the pin that held the cylinder ratchet, spun the barrel several times, then closed the breech and worked the action through two complete revolutions of the chamber, letting the hammer down with his thumb to avoid damage to the firing pin. Breaking the revolver again, Foxx wiped away the excess oil that remained on the blued metal surfaces that were exposed. Then he opened the fresh box of cartridges and reloaded the weapon, inspecting the nose and primer of each shell before slipping it into a chamber.

Satisfied finally, Foxx re-holstered the Smith & Wesson, and then gave his Colt House revolver the same treatment. When the stubby little Clover Leaf Colt was clean, with fresh loads in each of its four chambers, he returned the Colt to its holster-pocket inside his coat lapel. Then he strapped on the pistol-belt, slid his arms into the sleeves of his coat, set his hat firmly in place, and started for Pancake Jack's.

Lights were showing in most of the houses in the straggled line that stood silhouetted against the red sunrise sky on the east side of Sherman's street, but the only one with an open door was the squat, flat-roofed building that housed the restaurant. Foxx mounted the single step in front of the door. Then he stopped in the doorway, staring. Seated at the counter, pouring syrup on the hotcakes that steamed in the platter in front of him, was Abernathy.

Swallowing his surprise in a head-shaking gulp, Foxx straddled the stool next to the lawyer's and sat down. Abernathy turned to look at him.

"Well, good morning, Foxx," he said calmly, picking up his fork and holding it poised above his pancakes.

"Abernathy, would you mind telling me just where in the living hell you been?" Foxx asked, trying to match the other man's calmness.

"It's a long story." Abernathy cut a triangle out of the top hotcake of the stack and popped it into his mouth.

While the lawyer chewed, Foxx said, "You know I been looking for you all over the place, I guess."

Abernathy swallowed. "Why?"

"Why?" Foxx echoed. "Because you dropped outa sight like the earth had just opened up and swallowed you."

"I left in a hurry. I had a lot of traveling to do, and I didn't want to waste time trying to find you and tell you I was leaving."

A platter of pancakes grated across the counter in front of Foxx. At Pancake Jack's, no orders were required. The patrons knew they were going to get hotcakes with either ham or bacon, whichever of the two Jack happened to have on hand. This morning, strips of bacon flanked the stack of pancakes topped with a gob of fast-melting butter.

Foxx dug out the change to pay for his breakfast and handed it to the white-aproned proprietor who stood waiting. Jack dropped the two dimes in his apron pocket and produced a mug of coffee to place beside Foxx's platter.

After Jack had gone back to his griddle, Foxx ignored the tempting aroma of the coffee and bacon long enough to say, "When you get around to it, you might tell me where you traveled to and what taken you there."

"Topeka." Abernathy jerked his head toward the three men who sat at the far end of the counter; Foxx had not been consciously aware of them before. The lawyer went on, "I'll tell you all about it later,

when we're where we can talk privately. Right now
I'm going to finish my breakfast. I'm starved."

Foxx suddenly remembered that he was, too. He
began eating, glancing at Abernathy between bites.
The lawyer's white-linen collar was stained with
streaks of soot; his long coat was rumpled and wrinkled, as though it had been slept in. His face was
as grimed as his collar, and there was the stubble of
a day-old beard on his chin. Foxx smiled at the
usually dapper attorney's disheveled appearance, and
devoted himself to his food.

They finished breakfast and walked toward The
Union, their shadows on the dirt road stretching
away from them in elongated parallels under the
early morning sun.

Foxx looked at Abernathy through the blue veil
of smoke from his just-lighted stogie and suggested,
"This is about as private a place as we'll find. Why'd
you take off like a spooked jackrabbit for Topeka?
And how'd you get there and back so fast?"

"I had to go there because it's the capitol. And
I'm afraid I used your name pretty freely to make it
a quick trip. I hope I didn't get you into trouble
with the C&K."

"Whatever it was you done, I imagine I can live
with it. Go on, get down to cases. I got some news
for you, but it can wait till I find out what you
done."

"After that trouble the other day, and with Parsons
dead, I decided my clients had to have some kind
of legal protection," Abernathy began. "So, I went
looking for a judge who'd issue an injunction to keep
them from being dispossessed until there's a hearing

that'll settle the conflict between homestead claims and mineral claims."

"An injunction means nobody can throw 'em off," Foxx said thoughtfully. "Not even the C&K?"

"I'm afraid so. I'm sorry, Foxx."

"I take it that means you got one?"

"Only after a lot of trouble. I couldn't find a state judge who'd touch my petition. I finally got the injunction from the Federal district judge, and he's promised to back his writ with troops if the men here get out of hand again."

"I suppose that settles things, then. But, damn it, it sure looks to me like you put the C&K right in the soup."

"I'll try to help you work something out," Abernathy promised. "I don't know what it'll be, but I'll try."

They reached The Union and went inside. At that early hour of the morning, Bert had not yet opened the bar, but Sing, the Chinese "boy-of-all-work," was busy mopping the stairs. Foxx said, "I'd buy you a drink if Bert was here, or if I didn't have to wade through Sing's mopping to get my own bottle outa my room."

"It's a little soon after breakfast for me. Let's just sit over there in the corner out of Sing's way. Then, if anybody comes in, we'll go up to my room to finish our talk."

Abernathy led the way to a table in one corner. He and Foxx sat down. Foxx chose a chair that gave him a view of the balcony; he didn't know whether or not Burgin was still in his room, but he wanted to be able to see the gunman if he came out.

"You really must've cut a shuck to get to Topeka

and back so fast," he said to the lawyer. "I guess that's where you taken my name in vain?"

"I had to do that, Foxx. Getting there wasn't too much trouble. I hired a saddle horse from the livery-man here and rode to Dodge City, and took a Kansas Pacific rattler to Topeka. But the only way I could think of to get back fast enough was on your C&K spur."

Foxx was gazing at Abernathy in amazement, real-izing suddenly that he'd been underestimating the attorney. He also had a hunch what was coming next.

Abernathy said, "I suppose if you wanted to, you could have me disbarred for what I did."

"Don't borrow trouble till I've heard the whole story. Go on and finish."

"Well, I convinced the C&K district superintendent in Topeka that I was acting for you, and he arranged for what he called a bounce. It turned out to be just an engine and a caboose, and it lived up to its name. I've never had such a bumpy ride on a train in my life! It's all I can do to sit down."

"They do get a mite rough." Foxx smiled. "If I was you, I wouldn't worry about the train. I can smooth that over easy enough."

"I thought perhaps you could. But the injunction —well, I promise you I'll do my best to get your right of way cleared."

"Sure. To tell you the truth, Abernathy, I wasn't figuring to do much until things settled down here. Which won't be for a while yet, the way it looks now."

"I seem to get an impression that something impor-tant happened while I was gone."

"You left too soon. I'll skip over what don't signify too much, and start from last night. Frank Morse stayed over after the fight, got him a room upstairs here."

Abernathy nodded. "Yes. He does when there's a story he's working on."

"Bert rented Burgin the room next to Morse's. Last night, Morse heard Burgin talking to Homer Ingersoll, so he come down to my room and me and Romy—"

"Wait a minute!" Abernathy broke in. "I want to know how Ingersoll got into this. And who the devil is this Romy? Romy who? One of your men from the C&K?"

"Romy Dehon ain't with the C&K. She's a Pinkerton detective."

"A Pinkerton?" Abernathy's brow was furrowing when he started asking the question, and as the full meaning of Foxx's words sank home, his voice rose sharply. "She?"

Foxx nodded. "Yep. A woman Pinkerton. She worked with me on a stock swindle case up in Chicago a couple of years ago."

"My God!" Abernathy sighed. "The next thing you know, we'll have female policemen. Then lawyers. Even judges, I suppose." He sighed again. "All right, just give me a little time. I'll get used to the idea of a woman detective. Go on, Foxx."

Before Foxx could continue, Santa Fe Pete came in through the back door. He saw Foxx and Abernathy and crossed the floor to their table.

"By God, I knowed there'd be somebody over here that'll wanta hear what I found out," Pete began. "Foxx, you know—"

"Just a minute, Pete," Abernathy interrupted. "Foxx and I are talking serious business. We'll listen to your story later."

"I wasn't talkin' to you, lawyer," Pete said sharply. He turned back to Foxx. "Like I was about to say, Foxx—"

"Abernathy's right, Pete," Foxx said quickly. "We're in the middle of something real important, and we got to get on with it. Go have a drink and then we'll talk."

"I didn't come over here for a drink, damn it!" Pete retorted. "I got something important to say!"

"What you got to say'll just have to wait," Foxx told the old man, finality in his voice. "Come on, Abernathy. Let's go."

Without asking where they were going, Abernathy followed Foxx out of the saloon. On the street, the lawyer asked, "You don't mind telling me where we're going, I hope."

"Mainly out here so we can get away from Pete. I like the old fellow, but we got to get our heads together right away. It just struck me while we was trying to get Pete shut up that Romy'd better be in on what we figure to do."

"Be sensible, Foxx. What could a woman contribute to any decision we might make?"

"Morse told us both a few things you need to hear about. And Romy was with us when we listened to Burgin and Ingersoll talking. Ingersoll's put a price on you, Abernathy."

"Why? I never did anything to him!"

"It's too long to go into now. But Burgin's set to shoot you. Me, too, if I get in his way."

"That's ridiculous!"

"Not a bit. Wait'll you hear the whole story."

"I still don't see why we need your woman friend along," the lawyer objected.

"Don't misjudge Romy," Foxx cautioned. "She's a right savvy girl. I found that out when we was running down them fake C&K stock certificates."

Abernathy eyed Foxx narrowly. "You sound quite taken with this female detective. And I notice you referred to her as a girl. Young and pretty, I suppose?"

"She ain't what you'd call hard on your eyes. And she's got brains to go with her looks."

"I'm getting more and more anxious to meet her," the lawyer said dryly.

"You'll have your chance in about two minutes." Foxx snapped open his watchcase and looked at the time. "Breakfast's just about over with at the boardinghouse. Maybe we'll catch her before she gets away."

Romy was just getting up from the table when Foxx looked into the dining room. She frowned when she saw him. "Is something wrong, Foxx?"

"No. Abernathy's back."

"Where on earth has he been?"

"Topeka. I figured you oughta get in on the talk we got going, unless you got something else cooked up."

"Nothing at all. I was going to do a little prying on my own this morning, but I'm sure it's more important to join you and your friend." She hesitated. "Where can we go, though? Is there someplace where —"she looked around to make sure Mrs. O'Shea wasn't standing in the kitchen door—"we won't be noticed by anyone?"

"You said you rented a buggy to get here in. It's still at the livery stable, ain't it?"

"Of course."

"You and Abernathy take the buggy, then. I'll rent a saddle horse. We'll ride out from town a ways where nobody's likely to bother us."

"I'll get my coat and hat, and be ready in three minutes."

"You better come meet Abernathy first. He's out in the hall."

When Foxx introduced them, it was obvious to him, if not to Romy, that Abernathy was exercising a great deal of restraint to keep his skepticism from showing. The two bowed politely enough, though, and Romy immediately excused herself to go put on her hat and coat.

After she'd gone, Foxx looked questioningly at Abernathy. "Well?" he asked. "She meet your approval?"

"She's much better looking than I'd thought she'd be. And quite a bit younger."

"And smarter than you figure, too. You'll find that out."

"Where are we going?" The lawyer looked around the small square entry. "We certainly can't talk here."

"Romy's got a rig across the street at the livery stable. I'll go get it while she's putting on her hat."

"And where'll we go?"

"Anyplace. No place. Just far enough outa town so we can talk without worrying about Burgin."

"I still can't believe—"

"You will. Now, stop arguing. I'll rent a saddle

horse. You and Romy take the buggy. I'll ride shot-gun."

"You sound like you're taking Burgin seriously, Foxx."

"I am. You better, too. You will when you hear all of what we got to tell you." Foxx's voice was never more serious. "Now, you two be watching right inside the door, here. The minute I stop the buggy in front, get in and drive off. You follow me?"

"We'll be ready," Abernathy promised.

Foxx angled across the street to the livery stable. To save time he saddled the rented riding horse while the liveryman got the buggy ready. The entire operation took less than ten minutes.

Leading the buggy, his eyes flicking along the street, Foxx walked his mount back to the boarding-house. The street looked much as it did any morn-ing. There were two or three pedestrians, and a roan and a pinto pony at the hitch-rail in front of Pan-cake Jack's. Foxx bent in the saddle to take the lead-rope off the harness, then wheeled his horse to face the street and began scanning the opposite side.

As he'd promised, Abernathy was ready, but he was also conscious of the traditional role of a gentle-man. He walked with Romy to the right side of the buggy to hand her up to the seat. Romy had not settled down in the vehicle and Abernathy was walk-ing around the back of the buggy to reach the driv-er's seat when Foxx saw Burgin come out of Pancake Jack's.

At first glance, Foxx did not recognize the gunman. Burgin was not dressed as usual. He now wore duck pants and a plain tan shirt. The only recognizable article of his clothing was his hat. In the single quick glance, Foxx noticed that Burgin still carried his holstered gun low on his right hip.

Over his shoulder, trying to keep his eyes on Burgin, Foxx called, "Get moving, Abernathy! There's Burgin!"

Burgin saw Abernathy just as the lawyer was stepping up to the buggy's seat. The gunman's hand dropped by instinct to his hip, but seeing Foxx's eyes fixed on him, he stopped short of drawing. Foxx gave him no credit. The range was too great for accurate handgun shooting.

Abernathy finally got the reins in his hands and slapped them on the horse's back. The animal jerked forward. Abernathy wheeled the light, mobile buggy and started rolling toward Sherman's southern edge. Foxx reined his horse around to follow.

To look at the buggy, Foxx had to take his eyes off Burgin for a moment. When he twisted in the saddle to look back at Pancake Jack's, Burgin was gone. So was one of the saddle horses that had been standing at the hitch-rail.

Trusting that Abernathy would have the good sense to use the buggy whip and keep the horse moving straight ahead, Foxx angled across the street. Reason told him the only place Burgin could have gone was between the restaurant and the house next to it.

A moment later his guess was affirmed. He got a fleeting glimpse of Burgin between two houses. The gunman was using the houses for cover as he spurred to overtake the buggy, now just reaching the edge of town. Foxx kicked his mount's flanks to get a bit more speed out of the animal.

When the chase started, Foxx had been closer to the edge of town than Burgin, but Ingersoll's gunman had the advantage of knowing that the buggy must stay on the road, while Foxx was forced to search for Burgin's whereabouts.

As they came to the last houses and entered the flat open prairie, Foxx and Burgin were riding neck and neck. Foxx had a slight advantage; he was a score of yards closer to the buggy. The light vehicle was bouncing wildly now as it hit the rutted road beyond the town.

Foxx got little more than a glimpse of the buggy now that Burgin was in plain sight. Burgin's pinto was proving to be the faster horse of the two. The gunman was slowly drawing ahead of Foxx. Even though the range was extreme, Foxx let off a shot at Burgin. He saw the spurt of dust where the slug landed, far short of the speeding pinto's hooves.

Burgin raised his pistol when he heard the report of Foxx's Smith & Wesson, and Foxx took a tighter grip on the reins, ready to veer if he saw Burgin aiming at him. The buggy was the gunman's target, though. He rose from the saddle and stood in the reins to get a more positive sight and Foxx heard the report as Burgin triggered his weapon.

Foxx risked taking his eyes off Burgin for a moment to look at the buggy. Apparently the shot had missed, for the buggy still careened along the road and he could see the heads of both Abernathy and Romy in the seat.

A slug screamed past Foxx's head and he ducked instinctively. He'd been too intent on the buggy to notice that Burgin had narrowed the angle at which he'd been moving, then pulled rein for a second, just long enough to skid his mount's hindquarters and slow it for that one shot.

Foxx returned Burgin's fire just as the gunman
spurred ahead after the buggy again. Foxx's shot was
wide. Burgin tried for the buggy again, but his brief
pause to exchange slugs with Foxx had given the
buggy a few more yards' lead. Again the gunman's
bullet kicked up dust behind the swaying vehicle.

There was no way to get another ounce of speed
out of the livery horse, Foxx saw. He bent forward
and kept the beast at its full capacity, though by now
the horse's sides were beginning to heave. Burgin
was much closer to the buggy now. Foxx saw him
wrap the reins around his left hand, preparing for
another aimed shot, and tried vainly to make the
livery horse move faster.

A puff of powder smoke bloomed above the buggy
seat. Foxx saw Romy kneeling on the seat, her tiny
.22 gleaming in her hand. The unexpected shot from
the buggy caught Burgin off guard; he veered instead
of shooting and Foxx gained a few yards. Burgin
recovered quickly. He spurred after the buggy once
more, trying to regain the ground he'd lost.

Foxx had gained ground on Burgin when the gunman slowed and veered. He did some quick arithmetic. Burgin had two shots left, three if he carried
all his gun's chambers loaded. Foxx had a one-shot
edge; he'd used only two of the Smith & Wesson's
loads. He decided to hold the edge and concentrated
on getting in closer range.

A chuckhole in the rough road sent the buggy careening from side to side, and Foxx saw that Abernathy had been forced to rein in. Romy was still
kneeling in the buggy's seat, her popgun in her hand.
Burgin took advantage of the slower pace to which
the buggy had been forced; Foxx saw that he was

closing in fast. Somehow, he managed to get a bit more speed from his own horse, and the distance between him and Burgin was slowly closing.

Burgin looked back and saw Foxx gaining. He repeated the motion Foxx had noticed before, wrapping his reins around his hand in preparation to rein in quickly.

Foxx maintained his speed. He did not slow when Burgin skidded his mount momentarily and raised his weapon for another shot. Foxx heard the report and turned his attention from Burgin to the buggy. Foxx's eyes narrowed and his lips set in a grim line. He pounded his heels against his horse's flanks in a desperate effort to close the gap between him and Burgin. He was vaguely aware of Burgin's face turning his way and the gunman's revolver coming up.

Foxx paid no attention to the gun-muzzle swinging to cover him. Hot anger was flooding his brain. He glanced at the buggy again to be sure he'd seen right, and then bent low over the neck of his horse as the range between him and Burgin closed fast. His second glance had confirmed what he hadn't beileved when he'd looked before.

Abernathy was alone in the buggy. Romy no longer knelt on the seat beside him.

CHAPTER 16

Foxx was within range of Burgin now, but he still held his fire. The gunman fired and the whistle of his slug shrilled in Foxx's ear; he felt the bullet tug at his shoulder as it ripped through his coat. Burgin was reining in now, bringing his pistol up again, and Foxx realized that the killer must have a load in the sixth chamber of the revolver. Only the need to make his last shot count would lead the gunman to risk stopping with the range so close.

With a heavy hand, Foxx reined in his horse. He yanked the reins to his left as he pulled back on them. The animal's neck arched as it fought the bite of the bit in its mouth, but it slowed and swerved to give Foxx the free sight-angle he needed. He fired just as Burgin loosed his last remaining shot.

Foxx's trigger-finger was a split-second faster. Burgin's body arced as the slug from Foxx's Smith & Wesson tore into his chest. When Burgin's finger closed on the trigger, the muzzle of his gun was already dropping. Its slug thudded into the ground a few inches short.

Burgin slumped and his pistol fell from his hand. His head lolled loosely, pulling his shoulders forward. Arms dangling lifelessly, Burgin crumpled slowly, slid from the saddle, and sprawled beside the hooves of the pinto pony.

For the first time in several minutes Foxx had a chance to look ahead. The buggy was no longer rocking and bouncing now, the panicked horse finally responding to Abernathy's heavy hand on the reins.

Foxx nudged his panting horse with his toe and walked it to where Burgin lay. He leaned in the saddle long enough to make sure the gunman was dead, then toed the animal back into motion and caught up with the slowing buggy.

"Pull up!" he shouted as soon as he was close enough for Abernathy to hear him. Abernathy nodded without looking back, and Foxx caught up with the buggy as it creaked to a halt.

Abernathy dropped the reins and bent over Romy. Foxx could get only a glimpse of her body past the lawyer's shoulders. He swung out of the saddle. Abernathy was lifting Romy's limp form; Foxx hurried to help.

Between them, they raised Romy to the seat. Foxx was looking for bloodstains on her clothing to see how badly she was wounded when her eyes opened and her arms twitched. She brushed their hands away, grasped the back of the seat, and pulled herself erect.

"Let go of me, damn it!" she snapped. "I'm all right. I don't need any help!"

"You sure, Romy?" Foxx asked.

"Of course I'm sure! I've got a bump on my head where I hit the dash after the damned buggy threw me out of the seat, but I'm not hurt!"

Foxx and Abernathy stared speechlessly at one another for an instant before the relief flooding over Foxx brought its reaction. He burst into peals of loud, uncontrollable laughter.

"Shut up, damn you, Foxx!" Romy said angrily. "You don't have to laugh at me because I acted like a stupid amateur. It's not all that funny!"

"It ain't funny," Foxx managed to gasp between guffaws. "It sure is funnier than. what I looked to find, though. Hell, Romy, we was afraid you'd got killed!"

Romy stared at him for a moment, then began to smile. "Why, Foxx," she said. "I'm really flattered. I didn't know you cared that much about me." Then, before Foxx could answer, she asked quickly, "What about Burgin?"

"Dead, back on the road a ways."

"And you're all right?"

"Sure."

Romy noticed the rip in the shoulder of Foxx's coat. "You came awfully close to being back there with him. If that bullet had been a few inches lower—"

"It wasn't."

Abernathy broke in. "We came out here to talk about Burgin and Ingersoll," he pointed out. "There's no reason left for that now. The question is, where do we go from here?"

"Back to Ingersoll," Romy told him. "He's the one we'll have to deal with now."

"More than him, too, Abernathy," Foxx said.

"You're still a day behind what's happened. Tell you what, though. We can swap notes while we go back to town. I'll load Burgin's body on his nag, and we'll ride in slow and see what we come up with."

In the course of their slow three-mile ride back to town, Foxx and Abernathy and Romy exchanged a lot of information, but came to no agreement on a course of action. There wasn't any decision possible, they agreed, until the still-unresolved question of the rights of the prospectors could be settled.

"But your case is in real good shape," Foxx told Romy. "With a little boost from Abernathy and Morse, you can just about wind it up."

"It looks that way," she nodded. "But it's a shame, Foxx. You've done most of the work in breaking this thing open, and now you're going to get the least out of it."

"Well, there's no way to turn up aces back to back on every deal," Foxx shrugged philosophically. "The C&K's just held its own. We had a spur held up when I got here, and things ain't changed a bit. I'll wind things up and head on out, I guess."

"I haven't forgotten my promise," Abernathy told Foxx. "I intend to go out to the diggings today and try to get the men whose claims are on your right of way to let the construction go through."

"Sure. I'll appreciate it, Abernathy, but I don't look for much to come of it. Them prospectors ain't about to give up a good strike just to accommodate us."

Even before the little procession reached the livery stable to return the buggy and horses, a small crowd had begun to trail it, and minute by minute the crowd grew in number as word of the gunfight rippled through the town. Romy left almost at once to go to the boardinghouse to wash and clean up while the men waited for the barber to come and get Burgin's body.

Foxx and Abernathy were still answering the questions that came pouring from the curious when Santa Fe Pete pushed through the men gathered around them and took hold of Foxx's arm.

"I guess I was outa line, gettin' riled at you in the saloon," Pete said, his whiskers bristling. "And, by God, I still oughta be riled because you didn't ask me to give you a hand chasin' down this yazzabo. But I'd be obliged if you'll hold still and listen now."

"Looks like now's as good a time to tell me as any," Foxx replied. "Is it private or can all these folks hear what you got to say?"

"Hell, let 'em hear!" Pete replied. "Maybe they'll quit actin' like damn fools after I tell 'em this goldfield they're all so het up about don't amount to no more'n a hoss-turd."

"What're you getting at, Pete?" Foxx asked.

"What I been trying to tell everbody is that there ain't no gold lode out at them diggings, but I can't find nobody that'll listen to me!"

Abernathy heard Pete's statement and shook off the homesteaders who were trying to question him. He asked Pete, "Are you saying those prospectors didn't find any nuggets out at the diggings?"

"Oh, they found some gold, all right," Pete replied. "Only it wasn't nuggets."

"Hell, I seen some of them nuggets myself, Pete," Foxx put in. "And the men that dug 'em up had 'em tested with acid. What they found was gold, sure as God made little green apples."

"Damn it, I know that!" Pete retorted. "But I know where the gold come from. Me and my old partner, Jim Kileen, was the sonsabitches that put that gold there!"

"Why'd you do a thing like that?" Foxx asked.

"To save our goddamn scalps is why!"

"Wait a minute," Abernathy said. "I don't know what you're getting at, Pete, but I think I can tell when a man's telling the truth and when he's lying. And it doesn't sound to me like you're lying."

"This child don't lie, Mister Lawyer. Sure, I'll stretch out a tall tale now and agin to make it taller, but this ain't no tall tale. It's honest to God facts, and I can back it up!"

"Well, go ahead and do it, then!" one of the men in the crowd called out. "If it's the truth, maybe we'll see the end of them damn gold-grubbers and get back to having us a nice, peaceful town again!"

Foxx had been listening to the exchange between Abernathy and Santa Fe Pete. To him, too, Pete's words had the ring of truth. He raised his voice and said, "Wait a minute! If Pete's got a yarn to spin about that gold, then them men in the diggings oughta hear it the same time everybody else does!"

"Foxx is right about that!" Abernathy seconded.

Several voices from the crowd rose in agreement, then someone called out, "Let's go on out to the diggings, then!"

"How about it?" Foxx asked Pete. "You got anything against going along out there where everybody can listen to you at the same time?"

"Why, hell no!" Pete snorted. "Except I tried to

tell some of them yazzabos out there yesterday, and they wouldn't pay me no mind."

"They'll listen now, I promise you," Abernathy said firmly.

Within seconds the exodus had started. The crowd moved up the street. Doors opened and people came out to look, and then to join; the crowd grew larger. As it neared Mrs. O'Shea's, Foxx angled across and hurried inside, ignoring the landlady who stood on the porch.

Inside the door he called, "Romy!" When she appeared he said, "Come along!"

"Where to?"

"Don't stop to ask questions! Just come along!"

With a shrug, she obeyed. As they hurried to get to the front ranks of the group, he explained sketchily. She did not quite understand, but kept abreast of Foxx and Abernathy.

Down Sherman's main and only street the crowd surged, the noise of its approach preceding it. By the time the front ranks reached the northern edge of town, the prospectors were beginning to form in a mass behind the embankment. Most of them had brought their guns with them. Abernathy speeded up and ran ahead of the townspeople waving his arms.

"There's not any trouble," he shouted, his lawyer's voice pitched to override the rumble of the crowd's noise. "Put your guns down, men! All these folks want is for you to listen!"

"Listen to what?" one of the prospectors called.

"You'll find out quick enough!" Abernathy responded, climbing to the top of the earthen barrier.

Most of the prospectors recognized the lawyer, and counted him as being one of them. Their guns were slowly lowered and the two groups finally stood facing one another peacefully, although still somewhat suspiciously, across the barricade.

"Quiet down, everybody!" Abernathy shouted. When the hubbub of voices subsided, he went on, "There's a man here who's got something to tell you. I don't know exactly what he's going to say, but you'd better listen to him. My feeling is that what he's about to tell you is the truth. Pete, get on up here and finish your story!"

Santa Fe Pete scrambled up beside Abernathy. The lawyer slid down to leave him holding the spotlight. Pete took his time before starting, and when he began to speak, the crowd was as quiet as a well-behaved congregation in church.

"Now, I ain't good at makin' speeches, like the lawyer, here," he began. "But there ain't many of you folks that don't know me. I was here before your town got started. Them days, it warn't nothin' but prairie. All there was to see was bufflers and coyotes and Comanches and a bunch of wagon ruts mebbe two miles to the north, and them tracks was the Santa Fe Trail. Damn it, I helped make them tracks, haulin' goods in a four-mule wagon! It was mighty pritty country, then, and still is, I guess."

Pete paused and shook his head. "I guess I better quit ramblin' and get on with my yarn, only it ain't a yarn, it's what happened to me and my partner. Jim Kileen, he was, and Jim was a pretty good man. He's gone now. Him and me got caught in a blizzard and he taken a chill that carried him off. That was in fifty-four, and I buried him back along the Trail. I could show you the place today, was I a mind to."

After a pause to take a deep breath, the oldster went on.

"What I aim to tell you folks about begun in Santa Fe. It was in the summer of forty-six. Me and Jim had just finished up a haul there. It was later'n usual, and that was a year when the Comanches and Kioways was pestier'n usual, so wasn't too many wagons got through. We sold our load for a pretty fine price, I recall, after we'd dickered around a little bit with them storekeepers."

Pete was well launched now, and as Foxx listened to the old man he became one with the crowd. Everyone was giving the old man complete and sympathetic attention.

Pete's words weren't especially vivid, but they carried such a conviction of the event he'd lived through that his listeners seemed to feel they were standing beside Pete and Jim Kileen in the back room of Silvestrio Baca's store in Santa Fe, where they'd finally closed a deal for their wagon-loads of merchandise, as well as for the wagons and the mules that had pulled them from the banks of the Missouri River.

"We are agreed, then, *señores?*" the fat-faced Baca asked. He refilled their glasses from the bottle of Taos whiskey that rested between them on the counter. "I take all your goods, your wagons, and your mules, and I pay you seex thousan' American dollars. In gold, as you have want. *Verdad?*"

"We got a deal," Pete replied after looking at Jim for confirmation. "Except we keep our riding horses and two pack-mules."

"*Seguro que si,*" the merchant nodded.

Pete held out his glass; Baca touched it with the rim of his own, and all three drained their glasses to seal the bargain.

A balance scale stood on the counter; Baca pulled it closer to him and produced a strongbox from below the counter of his crowded store. Opening the steel chest, he began scooping out handfuls of coins, a mixture of gold and silver and copper that represented half the nations of the civilized world. French Napoleons and francs. Spanish doubloons and pieces of eight, Mexican pesos, United States eagles and double eagles, Portuguese escudos. British sovereigns, and still others clinked onto the wooden counter.

Pushing aside the coins of accepted value, the merchant refilled the teamsters' glasses and while Pete and Jim sipped and watched, he counted those of the major nations into separate heaps. He said, "You count after me, *señores*, but you will find there four thousand dollars. The rest, I weigh."

Pete and Jim refilled their own glasses this time while Baca weighed the gold coins of questionable face value. When he'd made three piles of assorted coins, Baca indicated them with a sweep of his hand. "This is make the seex thousand. We are like you say, even with *Estevan*, no?"

"Your count's always been good before, Baca," Pete said. "Now we got to do a mite of trading with you. We'll be needing grub to see us back to Saint Joe, and we swapped off our spare blankets when we was passing through Osage country and one of our nags went lame."

"We're plumb outa buckshot and low on powder, too," Kileen added. "We'll want about ten pounds of double-O shot and six bags of grain powder. And chawing terbaccer."

Baca refilled their empty glasses with the Taos lightning as he said, smiling, "*De gusto, señores.* Now I get some of my own money back from you, no?"

Pete and Jim started back that same day, taking the warm but less-used southern branch of the Santa Fe Trail, the Comanchero's route through the Canadian River valley to the flatland that began near the Texas border. There they angled northeast, fording the shallow headwaters of the Cimarron before turning north toward the Arkansas. It was the afternoon of the day they'd crossed the Cimarron that the Kiowas jumped them.

Kileen saw them first, sweeping up from a draw where the band had been lurking, about fifteen of them coming at full gallop. "We got trouble, Pete," he said, pointing.

Pete took a quick look back, then peered ahead. As far as he could see, the ground was flat as a table-top, with not a hillock or a draw in sight. He told Kileen, "We'll outrun 'em as long as the critters hold up. Then all we can do is stand."

From the beginning, it was an unequal race. The pack-mules did their best, but were far from approaching the speed of the Kiowa mustangs. The Indians gained steadily, closing the ground even after Pete and Kileen started using their Hall carbines. Battle-wise, the Kiowas scattered when the teamsters began shooting, so that Pete and Kileen soon stopped wasting their ammunition. The Kiowas were forming into a crescent to close on their outnumbered quarry when Pete saw the buffalo wallow.

"There's our cover," he called to his partner.

Kileen followed Pete's pointing finger and headed for the wallow. They reached it safely and wasted no time. Twisting the necks of their animals, they forced the horses and mules to lie flat in the shallow basin. Then they each took one side of the wallow to defend.

For more than two hours, the rifles held the Kiowa band out of bowshot, until Pete called to Kileen, "Toss me a sack of powder outa that pack in back of you, Jim. I'm runnin' low."

"I need some more, too," Kileen replied, rolling over to the pack-mule that lay behind him. He rummaged through the pannier and then said unhappily, "Damn it! There's only one bag in here, Pete, and it's half-empty."

"Where's them six sacks we bought off of Baca in Santa Fe?" Pete asked.

"Damned if I know. They jest ain't here. Neither is that new bag of buckshot."

Ignoring the Kiowas, the teamsters searched their pack-panniers and saddlebags. Except for another half-empty sack, they had no more powder, and no buckshot at all.

"Looks like we're up shit crick without no paddle, Pete," Kileen said thoughtfully. He shook his head dolefully. "Damn it, both of us musta been so drunk we walked outa Baca's place and left that powder and buckshot laying on the counter."

"I guess that's how it was," Pete agreed. He glanced over the rim of the buffalo wallow, and told Kileen, "Them Kiowas has figured something's wrong. They're closin' in."

"Damn me for a lousy drunk-ass pissant!" Kileen

gritted. "I was the one walked out and left that stuff!" He picked the sacks of gold coins that they'd taken out while searching for the powder and shot. "I picked up the money, but I left what we need right now a lot more'n we do gold!"

"It's as much my fault as yourn," Pete told his partner. "I had my eye on that money, too." He stopped short and then said thoughtfully. "Jim, all that gold ain't goin' to do us no good unless we get rid of them Kioways. Right now, there ain't much difference between it and lead, is there?"

"Except gold's worth—" Kileen began. He looked at Pete. "I don't see why it wouldn't work! Damn it, let's git busy!"

For the next few minutes, the partners worked furiously. Both of them wore old-style Bowie knives, the original Arkansas toothpicks, with stout twelve-inch blades. Using a packsaddle frame as a chopping block, they diced gold coins into buckshot-sized lumps, slashing the soft metal with hard, swift strokes that quickly gave them a sizable pile of irregular pellets.

After they'd diced a dozen handfuls of the odd-value coins, Pete called a halt. "We got all we need, looks like. And them Kioways is in range of our fukes, now. Let's give it a try."

Apparently, the failure of the two besieged men to keep firing had puzzled the Kiowas. They took no chances of being tricked by what they might have assumed to be a new white man's battle stratagem. When Pete and Kileen peered over the side of the wallow, the Indians had encircled the depression and were belly-crawling toward them.

Pete and Kileen had loaded the fukes heavily. The guns were those used by the early Plains' buffalo hunters: double-barreled ten-gauge sawed-off shot-guns. Popping up, the two whites picked targets and fired. Four fast shots accounted for four Kiowas.

Reloading swiftly, the pair fired again and managed a third quick volley before the Kiowas broke. Reloading for a last time, Pete and Kileen chased the running Indians on foot, accounting for three more at a distance from the wallow before the Kiowas reached their horses and fled.

"We counted up later," Pete concluded the account of the fight, looking down on the upturned faces of his spellbound audience, who by now were reliving those tense moments with the old man. "Me and Jim shot four times apiece with them fukes, and we let go with both barrels ever time we pulled trigger. I reckon we musta shot away near a pound of gold before them Kioways taken off."

He paused, suspended somewhere between past and present, then in a quietly positive tone, went on. "Now, all them bits and pieces of gold didn't go into Kioways. Them old fukes spread a wide pattern; their load begun to scatter damn near when it left the muzzle. And most of them little chunks of gold must've got buried in the ground. And that buffler waller was right over yonder, not fifteen feet from where we're standin' now."

In the stillness that fell on the throng when Santa Fe Pete stopped talking, Ben Mercer called, "You're saying there ain't no lode here? Is that it?"

"That's it, all right," Pete replied. "What little gold's in the ground here's what me and Jim put there nigh onto thutty years ago. And you got my word that's the gospel truth."

"How do we know this is the same place, old man?" one of the prospectors asked. "Places around here look pretty much alike."

"Friend," Pete said solemnly, "if it was you that'd been savin' your scalp that day, would you have forgot the place where it happened? Even if it was thutty weeks or thutty years or fifty?"

After a thoughtful pause, the man who'd asked the question shook his head. "No," he replied. "I guess not."

"Well, I ain't, neither," Pete said. "Now, I told you the true story about how that gold got put here. You can go on digging as long as you live. You can dig on down clean to the gates of hell, but you ain't gonna find no more."

Ben Mercer's question had fractured the spell that had held the crowd; the second question and Pete's answers demolished it. A babble of voices broke out. Prospectors and miners alike began breaking into little knots to discuss the situation.

Foxx said to Romy and Abernathy, "We might as well get back to town. I got a feeling that's all she wrote. That bunch of prospectors won't be here much longer, a day or two, maybe a week at best."

"Yes," Abernathy agreed. "And even if a lot of them were my clients, I can't say I'm completely sorry. Just the same, I'd better go over there and tell Ben and his friends they were about to win, even if they did lose first." He started for the diggings, leaving Foxx and Romy standing alone.

Romy looked at the crowd beginning to scatter now. A few of the prospectors were already beginning to pack their gear in preparation for leaving.

She said, "It's too bad to see hopes broken up. Sad, in a way, but their hopes never were very solid, were they?"

She tucked her hand into Foxx's elbow and they began walking slowly back toward the street. Foxx said thoughtfully, "Both of our cases is wound up now, or will be in a day or so. Frank Morse can give you anything you need to fill in."

"Yes. I can turn Ingersoll over to the Justice Department attorneys now." She sighed. "I do hate the idea of jouncing by myself in that buggy all the way back to Fort Dodge, though."

"There'll be a C&K supply train pulling up at railhead tomorrow or next day. I could give you a lift, if you don't mind riding with me in the caboose."

"Thank you, Foxx." Romy squeezed his arm. "Or did you know I was just waiting for you to invite me?"

Arm in arm, they continued walking down the dusty street, only now both Foxx and Romy were smiling.

AN OCCULT NOVEL OF UNSURPASSED TERROR

EFFIGIES

BY William K. Wells

Holland County was an oasis of peace and beauty . . .

until beautiful Nicole Bannister got a horrible package that triggered a nightmare,

until little Leslie Bannister's invisible playmate vanished and Elvida took her place,

until Estelle Dixon's Ouija board spelled out the message: I AM COMING—SOON.

A menacing pall settled over the gracious houses and rank decay took hold of the lush woodlands. Hell had come to Holland County —to stay.

A Dell Book $2.95   (12245-7)

Dell Bestsellers

- [ ] **SHOGUN** by James Clavell $3.50 (17800-2)
- [ ] **JUST ABOVE MY HEAD**
  by James Baldwin $3.50 (14777-8)
- [ ] **FIREBRAND'S WOMAN**
  by Vanessa Royall $2.95 (12597-9)
- [ ] **THE ESTABLISHMENT** by Howard Fast $3.25 (12296-1)
- [ ] **LOVING** by Danielle Steel $2.75 (14684-4)
- [ ] **THE TOP OF THE HILL** by Irwin Shaw $2.95 (18976-4)
- [ ] **JAILBIRD** by Kurt Vonnegut $3.25 (15447-2)
- [ ] **THE ENGLISH HEIRESS**
  by Roberta Gellis $2.50 (12141-8)
- [ ] **EFFIGIES** by William K. Wells $2.95 (12245-7)
- [ ] **FRENCHMAN'S MISTRESS**
  by Irene Michaels $2.75 (12545-6)
- [ ] **ALL WE KNOW OF HEAVEN**
  by Dore Mullen $2.50 (10178-6)
- [ ] **THE POWERS THAT BE**
  by David Halberstam $3.50 (16997-6)
- [ ] **THE LURE** by Felice Picano $2.75 (15081-7)
- [ ] **THE SETTLERS**
  by William Stuart Long $2.95 (15923-7)
- [ ] **CLASS REUNION** by Rona Jaffe $2.75 (11408-X)
- [ ] **TAI-PAN** by James Clavell $3.25 (18462-2)
- [ ] **KING RAT** by James Clavell $2.50 (14546-5)
- [ ] **RICH MAN, POOR MAN** by Irwin Shaw $2.95 (17424-4)
- [ ] **THE IMMIGRANTS** by Howard Fast $3.25 (14175-3)
- [ ] **TO LOVE AGAIN** by Danielle Steel $2.50 (18631-5)

At your local bookstore or use this handy coupon for ordering: —

Dell **DELL BOOKS**
P.O. BOX 1000, PINEBROOK, N.J. 07058

Please send me the books I have checked above. I am enclosing $ _____
(please add 75¢ per copy to cover postage and handling). Send check or money
order—no cash or C.O.D.'s. Please allow up to 8 weeks for shipment.

Mr/Mrs/Miss _____

Address _____

City _____ State/Zip _____